Sta____

Ellen Schwartz

CEDARLAND SCHOOL
LIBRARY

ELLEN SCHWARTZ

POLESTAR
BOOK PUBLISHERS

Starshine on TV
Copyright © 1996 by Ellen Schwartz

No part of this publication may be reproduced, stored in a
retrieval system or transmitted, in any form or by any
means, without prior permission of the publisher or, in
case of photocopying or other reprographic copying, a
licence from CANCOPY (Canadian Copyright Licensing
Agency), 6 Adelaide Street East, Suite 900, Toronto,
Ontario, M5C 1H6.

Polestar Book Publishers
1011 Commercial Drive, Second Floor
Vancouver, BC
Canada   V5L 3X1

The publisher would like to thank the Canada Council,
the British Columbia Ministry of Small Business, Tourism
and Culture, and the Department of Canadian Heritage for
their ongoing financial assistance.

Cover illustration and design by Jim Brennan
Editing by Suzanne Bastedo
Printed in Canada by Hignell Printers Ltd.

Second printing January 1997

CANADIAN CATALOGUING IN PUBLICATION DATA
Schwartz, Ellen, 1949-
    Starshine on TV

ISBN 1-896095-13-5
    I. Title. II. Title: Starshine on television
PS8587.C578S835 1996   jC813'.54   C96-910011-6
PZ7.S4974St 1996

For Audrey

*Thanks to Alex Downie,
Karen Needham, Cynthia Pollock,
Kent Harrison, Duncan Rayside
and Len Kirschner.*

Author's Note

The *Nephila,* or golden web spider, referred to in this book is a real spider. For readers who would like to learn more about spiders, I recommend *Spiders and Their Kin* by Herbert W. Levi and Lorna R. Levi (Golden Press) and *Amazing Spiders* by Claudia Schnieper (Carolrhoda Books Inc.).

Readers familiar with the first two Starshine books may notice a difference in the spelling of *Nephila.* In the earlier books, it was spelled *Nephilia.* While doing research for this book, I discovered that *Nephila* is the correct spelling. I apologize for the error.

Chapter One

"I'm a little teapot, short and stout,
Here is my handle, here is my spout ..."

I dropped my school bag on a kitchen chair and went through to the living room. There was Peggy, my little sister, in the middle of the room, one hand on her hip, the other arm bent to the side like the spout. My parents were sitting on the couch, watching. Grinning. Beaming.

My mom turned, then patted the couch beside her. I didn't sit down. I wasn't interested in Peggy Shapiro's Show-off Hour. Every day she gave a recitation of what she'd done at preschool. She sang all the songs. She danced all the dances. She presented all the artwork. My parents ate it up. It was disgusting.

"When I am all empty, I will shout,
'Tip me over and pour me out!'"

Peggy leaned to the side, straightened up and bowed. My parents clapped. Peggy grinned.

"That was terrific, Pumpkin!" my mom said.

"What talent!" my dad said.

"Wasn't she good, Star?" my mom asked.

"Wonderful."

"Gretchen said I sung so good, I could be milk monitor tomorrow," Peggy announced.

"Milk monitor!" my dad exclaimed. "That's an important job." He held out his arms and Peggy jumped in. He had his goggles pushed up on his forehead — he must've been working when Peggy came home. My dad's a stained glass artist and my mom's a potter, and their studio is in the house.

Peggy pulled off the goggles, then put them on herself. They slipped down to the tip of her little button nose. "How do I look, Daddy?"

My dad chuckled. "Adorable! Doesn't she look adorable, Joanie? Star?" He stood up with Peggy in his arms. "Let's go show you how cute you look in my goggles." He walked out, Peggy giggling.

My mom turned to me. "How was school, Star?"

"Fine." Of course, I didn't learn a new song or get chosen to be milk monitor. I was turning to go up to my room when the doorbell rang. "I'll get it," I called.

A guy in a courier's uniform was there. "Starshine Shapiro?"

"That's me."

"Special delivery. Sign here."

I signed and he handed me a small package. In it was a small glass bottle. The cork lid had air holes punched in it. A label said, LIVE SPECIMEN. AMERICAN ASSOC-

IATION OF ARACHNOLOGY. "Hooray! It's finally here!" I said, closing the door. I peeled the label off the jar. Inside, a small spider sat on a moist wad of cotton. A female — I could tell from the markings.

"What's finally here?" my mom said, coming up behind me.

"My nymph."

"Your what?"

"My spider that I've been waiting for."

My mom backed away. "It's not poisonous, is it?"

"No, it's a *Nephila.*"

"*Nephila*? Like Goldie?"

"Hey, you remembered!" Goldie was a *Nephila* spider that my mom accidentally brought home from the fruit store in a bag of papayas a couple of years ago. Goldie laid eggs on our back porch, and when they hatched, it was big news in the spider world because *Nephilas* are tropical and it was the first known hatching of *Nephila* eggs in the Northern Hemisphere. (My parents haven't been able to eat papayas since.)

My mom peered at the glass vial. "That doesn't look like Goldie."

"It's not an adult yet."

"What is it, a teenager?"

"Hilarious, Mom."

She grinned. "I thought so."

"The nymph is the stage before adult," I explained. "It has to moult one more time, and then it'll be all grown up."

"And then?"

"And then I start my experiment. Oh, I'm so excited, I can't wait!"

"What experiment is this?"

"WHAT EXPERIMENT? Mom, I told you and Dad all about it the other night, don't you remember?"

My mom looked sheepish. "Ummm ..."

"You weren't listening!"

"Tell me again."

"You'd better listen this time." Oh, I loved this.

"I promise."

I sighed and rolled my eyes as if it was an ordeal to go through it again, but the truth was, I loved talking about the experiment. In fact, I loved talking about anything to do with spiders. "OK. The American Association of Arachnology is having a contest for kids, to see who can grow the strongest *Nephila* web."

"What for?"

"To make it even stronger than it already is."

"Is it strong?"

"Is it strong!" I repeated. "It's one of the strongest spider webs in the world. People use it to carry stuff in. Like, in New Guinea, they use *Nephila* webs as fishing nets."

"Really?"

"Really."

"Fish?"

"Fish."

"So if the web is so strong already, why make it stronger?"

"'Cause then it could hold even more. People could use

it as a grocery bag. You know, like those cloth bags you take to the store. And then people would use fewer plastic bags. And that would be good for the environment."

She grinned. "Hey, that's a terrific idea! An organic, biological, environmentally friendly grocery bag." My mom's an environment freak. She even recycles waxed paper. Our kitchen is filled with rinsed-off squares of waxed paper clothespinned to strings, drying out. If you're not part of the solution, you're part of the problem, my mom always says.

"Well, as I always say, if you're not part of the solution —"

"I know, Mom, I know," I interrupted. "Oh, can't you just see it? Millions of people going to the store with beautiful bright yellow *Nephila* web bags?"

"It would certainly make grocery shopping more colourful." She paused. "So how are you going to make the web stronger?"

"Well, that's the whole idea of the experiment," I said. "Each week, for six weeks, I'll feed my spider a different kind of bug. And each week I'll test the web to see how much weight it can hold."

"How are you going to do that?"

"With golf balls."

"Golf balls?"

"Don't worry, I've got it all figured out."

"Golf balls?"

"Mom."

"OK, so you test the web. And then?"

"And then at the end of six weeks I send in my results and the American Association of Arachnology figures out who got the strongest web. Just think, Mom, I could be the person who finds the perfect bug! I could save the environment! Or at least get rid of plastic grocery bags."

"Is there a prize?"

"That's the best part," I said. "It's a beautiful full-colour wall poster of a *Nephila* spider in a papaya tree!"

A couple of days later, the *Nephila* moulted. Since *Nephilas* are tropical, I'd been keeping the glass vial on my windowsill where the nymph would be near warmth and light. I'd moistened the cotton a few times so that she didn't get too dry. I'd also offered her a few flies, but she didn't bite. That was OK. Spiders can go a few days without eating.

Julie, my best friend, was over when I noticed that the nymph's exoskeleton had started cracking. "Julie!" I called. "Julie, come here!"

Julie was on the other side of my room, at the mirror. She was putting a beard on herself. Not a real one. A fake one, made of wispy grey cotton from her Stage Makeup Kit. Last year, in grade four, Julie and I won a contest in our school for the best play about a myth. Our play was about Arachne, the Greek maiden who was turned into a spider by the goddess Athena, who was jealous of Arachne's weaving. I was Arachne and Julie was Athena. Anyway, we won some prize money, and Julie spent hers on this makeup kit since she wants to be an actress when she grows up. She's forever going around with purple eye shadow and fake noses and bloody gashes. Today it was a beard. She had attached the cotton to her face with glue and teased it out to look beardish. Only she'd pulled it too far and it was halfway down her chest and she was trying to push it back up but it wasn't working. "Help!" she said. "I look like a one-hundred-year-old elf."

"Julie! Get over here!" I shouted.

"Get back there, you," Julie grumbled, trying to scrunch up the beard. It didn't work. Now the beard stretched almost to her waist.

"Julie — quick — oh, you missed it!"

"What?" She looked over my shoulder, covering me with beard.

"The spider. It moulted. See the exoskeleton?"

"Where? What? That crumply shell thing?"

"Crumply shell thing!"

"Sorry."

"Oh, look at her, Jule. Isn't she beautiful?"

"She? How do you know it's a she?"

"'Cause she's big and colourful. See how long her abdomen is? See those stripes? And the white spots? That's a female. The males are small and brown and boring-looking."

Julie grinned. "Right on, girls!"

"Come on, let's show her her new home." We went out to the back porch, to the corner where a pipe came out of the house. My parents' workshop is just on the other side of the wall and the pipe carries the extra heat from my mom's kiln. This was the exact spot where Goldie had lived, and I was pretty sure it was the heat from the kiln that had kept her alive — after all, the *Nephila* is a tropical spider and likes to be cosy and warm. I hoped my new spider would be happy in the corner spot, too.

I shook the spider out of the vial. She crawled right to the corner. "See? She likes it," I told Julie, who was watching from a distance in case the spider decided to crawl in her direction. "Oh, this is a good sign, I know it!"

Julie came a little closer.

"What should we call her?" I said.

"How about Goldie the Second?"

I shook my head. "It would make her feel like she's second best."

Julie thought for a minute. "Neffie?"

I rolled my eyes. "Julie."

"Webbie?"

"Julie!"

"OK, OK. They spin a gold-coloured web, right?"

"Right."

"OK. Gold ... Golden ... How about Goldilocks?"

"She doesn't have hair, for goodness sake!"

"Well ..."

We both thought. I watched the spider. She started moving and a golden strand of silk floated from her abdomen, near her rear leg. Julie and I turned to each other and said at once, "Goldy-legs!"

"Perfect!"

"Now," I said, "let's go get Goldy-legs some lunch."
"Can I take my beard off first?"

FRED'S BAIT SHOP, said the sign in the window.
EARTHWORMS. GRUBS. FISHING TACKLE. TERRARIUM
SUPPLIES. FRIENDLY SERVICE.

"Fred's bait shop?" Julie said, realizing where we were.
"Aren't we going to the park and you look under benches
while I swing?"

"Julie, this is a scientific experiment. I can't use any old
bugs. And besides, I need a week's worth at a time."

"A store full of bugs?" She shuddered. "I'm not going in
there!"

"But Julie —"

"I'll wait for you out here."

"This could take a while."

"I don't care. I'll peel the glue off my chin while I'm
waiting."

"OK," I shrugged, and went inside.

At first all I saw was fishing stuff. One entire wall of the
store was full of fishing rods. Another wall was full of
reels. A display case contained fishing hooks. Then I
noticed that the middle of the store was full of cages and
jars filled with insects. I wandered down the aisle. The
cockroaches were crawling over each other. The flies
banged against the screen walls, fell down, buzzed around
and banged into the walls again. Praying mantises clung
to twigs, so still you couldn't tell where they left off and

the twigs began. One tank just seemed to be full of dirt, but then the dirt rippled, as if tiny underground earthquakes were happening, and I realized the dirt was full of earthworms.

"Can I help you?"

I turned. A man was looking at me. He had a reddish brown mustache and was wearing a red-and-blue-plaid flannel shirt with the sleeves rolled up. His button said: HI, I'M FRED. CAN I BUG YOU?

I laughed. "I like your button."

Fred smiled. "Thanks. Were you looking for something special?"

"Well … you see … I have a pet spider and I need something to feed her."

"What does your spider like?"

He didn't smirk or make it sound like I was some loopy kid. I liked that.

"I don't know," I said. "I just got her. She's a *Nephila*—"

"A *Nephila!*" he said. "The tropical spider?"

I *really* liked this guy.

I nodded. "See, I'm doing this experiment …" I told him all about it.

"No kidding!" he said. "Grocery bags. Great idea."

I grinned at him. "So what do you think I should get?"

Fred scratched his head. "Gee, I don't know. I've never fed a *Nephila* before."

"Well, I guess it should be some kind of flying insect, since that's what *Nephilas* usually eat."

"Is it?"

I nodded. "They spin their webs and wait for their food to fly into it."

"Yes, of course, they're orb-weavers, aren't they?"

"Right."

"OK, let's see now ... flying insect ... hmmm ..."

We wandered side by side, peering into cages. Moths ... wasps ... flies ... katydids ... We stopped in front of the cockroach cage. They were big. They were black. They were shiny. Fred and I looked at each other. "What do you think?" he said.

"They'd be a mouthful, that's for sure."

"Start your experiment off with a crunch."

I grinned. "I'll take a week's worth."

Fred went over to the cockroach cage, scooped a handful into a jar and screwed a screen lid onto the jar. "I'd guess that's enough. If you run out, come back and I'll throw in some more."

"OK. Thanks."

I paid Fred. As I turned to go he said, "Say, listen, let me know how your experiment goes, OK?"

I grinned at him as I crossed my fingers for luck. "You bet."

"Cockroaches!" Julie shrieked. The right side of her chin was clean, but there were still patches of glue on the left side.

"Just this week," I said. "Next week it'll be something else." I held out the jar. "You want to come and watch me feed Goldy-legs the first cockroach?"

"Get that away from me!" she yelled, backing away.

"I'll let you feed it to her. Since you're my best friend and all."

"Away! Away!"

"But Julie, you're missing your chance to take part in an important experiment. An experiment that could make history —"

"AWAY!"

"Are you sure?"

"Starshine, there's one thing I'm perfectly sure of, and that is, if you don't get those cockroaches away from me, my lunch is going to end up all over you."

Now it was my turn to back away. "Blech!" I hid the jar behind my back. "Don't you dare throw up on my cockroaches."

"I'm trying not to!"

We glared at each other for a minute, then burst out laughing. "Oh, Starshine, you weirdo," Julie said.

"Oh, Julie, you sicko."

"Good luck with your experiment."

"Good luck with your chin."

"My what?" She put up her hand. "Oh yeah. I'd better go home and wash my face."

Julie turned down the street and I headed home. When I got there, I went out to the porch, plucked a cockroach from the jar and placed it on the edge of the web. For a second, the bug just sat there. In that second, Goldy-legs glided across the web. The cockroach scuttled away, but it was too late. Goldy-legs grabbed it and started wrapping it in silk. Soon it was a little golden bundle. Then she bit the cockroach, paralyzing it. She waited a moment, then crushed it with her teeth, pouring in juices that turned the cockroach's body to liquid. She sucked it up like a milkshake. By the time she'd finished, there was just a little heap of hard body parts left over.

I breathed a sigh of relief. Goldy-legs had a healthy appetite. My experiment was off to a good start.

At the end of the week I called Julie to come over for the historic first weigh-in.

"No more cockroaches?"

"No more cockroaches."

"I'll be right over."

I was setting things up when she got there. I had swiped some of Peggy's Tinker Toys. I made two H's with them, with the tall parts a little closer together at the top and a little wider apart at the bottom, so they would stand up. Next to them I had a bowl of golf balls.

Julie pointed to the H's. "What are those?"

"The weighing posts."

"And those?"

"Golf balls."

"I know they're golf balls! What are they for?"

"You'll see."

Now for the tricky part. I had to get Goldy-legs out of her web and get the web off the wall and onto the weighing posts — all without killing her or wrecking the web.

I nudged Goldy-legs with my finger. Startled, she moved away. I nudged her again, and she scurried farther. One more push, and she was out of the web. Quickly I pulled it away from the porch wall. It felt a little bit sticky. Holding my fingers apart, I carried it to the table and gently lowered it onto the four corners of the weighing posts. I hardly breathed. It was like transferring a cat's cradle from your fingers to someone else's — one slip and the whole thing would unravel.

Slowly, I pulled my fingers away. The web held. "Whew!" I said.

"What about poor Goldy-legs?" Julie said. "She's homeless now."

"She'll be OK. She'll spin another web. It's like with birds. If you take eggs away from a mother bird, she'll lay more."

"Hey, cool."

"Come on, it's time for the big test." Gently I laid a golf ball in the web. It stretched a little, but held.

"So that's what those are for!" Julie said.

I smiled at her and put another golf ball in the web. It sagged a bit more but still held. Carefully I added a third ball. "Three ... four ... hold! hold!" I whispered. "Five ..." Clonk, clonk, clonk, clonk, clonk! The web tore and all the balls bounced out.

"Awww, too bad," Julie said.

"Hey, it's only her first web," I said. "Maybe she's still

getting the hang of weaving. I bet even Arachne didn't weave so great the first time." I handed Julie a sheet of paper and a pencil. "Here, you be the official recorder."

"RECORD OF WEB STRENGTH," Julie read aloud and then filled it in.

WEEK: 1
DIET: Cockroaches
OF GOLF BALLS BEFORE BREAKING: 4
TOTAL WEIGHT:

"How do you figure out total weight?" Julie said.

"Well, each golf ball weighs about fifty grams," I said. "So four times that is two hundred."

Julie wrote "200" on the Record of Web Strength and I gathered up the weighing posts and golf balls.

"That was exciting," Julie said. "All that suspense. Will the web hold? Will it break? How many golf balls? Will this be the one? How far can the web stretch? Tension fills the room — I mean, the porch —"

I laughed, then said, "I think I'll try flies next week. Those crispy little delicious wings might do the trick, don't you think?"

"BLECH!"

Chapter Two

CONSERVATORY CLOSED
FILMING IN PROGRESS
SORRY FOR THE INCONVENIENCE

said a big sign in front of the Bloedel Conservatory.

"Closed?" I said, braking my bike to a stop. I looked round at my mom. "CLOSED? After I rode all the way up here? After I practically killed myself?" I clutched my chest. "How could they do this to me?" I slid off my bike and flopped to the ground tragically.

My mom laughed, wiping her forehead. "Oh, come on, Star, it wasn't that bad. Anyway, you need the exercise."

I just sniffed. OK, it wasn't *that* bad, but it was still a haul. My mom and I ride up here to the Bloedel Conservatory in Queen Elizabeth Park every week, up this monster hill. We come to visit Charlie, the salmon-crested cockatoo. He's our favourite bird. Charlie gets all excited when we come. His crest turns bright orange and he bobs his beak up and down and he hops over and cocks his head and squawks as if to say, "Hi, there!" But he wouldn't squawk today.

"Charlie'll miss us," I said, sitting up. "He'll be lonely."

"I'm sure he doesn't even remember we exist when we're not there," my mom said.

"I bet he's pining away for us right now."

"I bet he's flirting with the film crew."

I gave her a disgusted look. "Come on, let's go see what they're filming," I said.

We pressed our faces against the Conservatory glass and looked inside. There were two huge cameras on wheels and lots of people with clipboards and earphones. There was a guy who was waving his arms and looking like he was telling everybody what to do. I guessed he was the director. A man and woman were sitting in a hammock in front of the cameras. The woman had on what looked like a nightgown, purple with yellow flowers. The man was wearing one of those safari hats, with a strap under his chin. Charlie was perched in a tree behind them. His pale pink feathers looked beautiful against the green leaves, and his orange crest jutted up like a fan.

"I wonder how he got up there," I said to my mom. The little birds fly around inside the Conservatory, but the big birds have their wing feathers clipped so they won't bash into the glass. Usually Charlie just hops around.

"I guess they lifted him up for the film," my mom said.

"I hope he's not dizzy," I said. "He's not used to heights."

A guy came out from the side with one of those movie

chalkboards. It said SWELTERING SAFARI, SCENE 9, TAKE 4. He snapped the top of the chalkboard and scurried out of the way. The couple moved their faces together like they were going to kiss. Blech. I can't stand seeing people kiss in movies.

Suddenly, Charlie jerked his head in our direction. He stretched out his wings. Then he swooped down from the tree, right in front of the lady's face, his wings beating the air, heading straight for my mom and me. He lurched a bit, as if he wasn't used to flying. Someone yelled, "Cut!" Charlie started sinking, but he kept on coming. "Look, Mom, he sees us!" I said.

"Oh, no," my mom said.

"He recognizes us."

"Oh, no!"

"I told you he'd miss us."

"OH, NO!"

Charlie flew straight into the glass — WHOMP! — and fell down on the Conservatory floor. He lay there in a heap.

"Charlie!" I yelled, flinging open the door. I didn't care if the Conservatory was closed, this was an emergency. I ran to Charlie. He lay motionless, but his eyes were open. "Charlie, don't die!" I said, stroking his wing.

"Starshine, you're not supposed to be in here," my mom whispered, following me inside.

"Charlie, come back, please, Charlie ..." I crooned.

Charlie swiveled his head and nipped my finger.

"He's alive!" I shouted. "Oh, Charlie, you're alive!"

Charlie jumped to his feet, ruffled out his feathers and settled them down again. He looked at me with one eye and squawked.

By now, everyone had come running.

"What's going on?"

"Who are these people?"

"I'm sorry, we're filming here."

"That crazy bird!"

My mom tried to explain that Charlie must have recognized us through the glass. The movie people didn't believe her, but luckily Alex, the supervisor, stuck up for us and said it was true, we did come every week. Meanwhile Charlie was hopping around and squawking like crazy.

"I'm terribly sorry," my mom said. "We didn't mean to disrupt your filming. Come on, Starshine, let's go."

Everybody went back to their places except the director. "What's your name, young lady?" he said to me.

Uh-oh, I'm in trouble now, I thought. I gulped. "Starshine Shapiro."

"She really didn't mean —" my mother began.

"How old are you, Starshine?" he said.

He wants to see if I'm old enough to go to jail! I thought in a panic. "Ten and three-quarters."

"Honestly," my mom started again, "we had no idea —"

"Perfect!" he said.

"What?" my mom and I said together.

"Could we speak for a moment?" he said to us. "Outside?"

"S-sure," I said.

CEDARLAND SCHOOL
LIBRARY

"Take five," he called, and the three of us went outside the Conservatory. He stuck out his hand and shook first my mom's hand, then mine. "I'm Richard Brintmorgan, the director of *Sweltering Safari*." He pulled a card out of his shirt pocket and handed it to my mom. *Richard Brintmorgan*, it said in fancy writing. *Director. Agent. Talent Scout.*

Mr. Brintmorgan leaned down to me. "Starshine, how'd you like to be on TV?"

"TV?" I said.

"TV?" my mom said.

"TV," he said. "You see, I don't only do feature films, I do commercials, too. I have a new client, Kitten Krunchies cat food, and I've been looking for a child actor —"

"Starshine's not an actor," my mom said.

"I am so!" I turned to Mr. Brintmorgan. "Me and Julie — that's my best friend — won first prize last year in a school contest for 'The Story of Arachne.' I was Arachne."

"Starshine," my mom began.

"Julie was Athena," I added, so he wouldn't think Julie didn't have an important part, too."

"Well, that's just dandy," he said. "But really, acting experience isn't necessary. It's more a quality — a look, a presence, and of course a real concern for animals. Which Starshine obviously has, the way she hovered over that bird in there."

"Charlie," I said.

"Right. Charlie." He turned to my mom. "I'm sure you think this is a put-on, Mrs. Shapiro, my spotting Starshine just like that. But believe me, after years in the business, you get a nose for talent. And she's got it, I can tell. Real presence."

I smiled as sweetly as I could.

"And I'll bet you're just as natural with cats as you are with cockatoos, right, Starshine?"

I tried to think if I was. It was weird — I couldn't think of many times I'd been with cats. Dogs, lots of times. Julie has a poodle, Roxy, who follows me everywhere. Mrs. Wentworth next door has a black lab named Hughie and I play with him all the time. But cats? I didn't seem to have been around cats much. Except at Lucy Chatham's birthday party, when her cat kept hanging around and I kept sneezing. I must have had a cold that day.

"I get along great with dogs," I said hopefully.

"Excellent!" Mr. Brintmorgan. "I'm sure you'll get along great with cats, too. Now, Mrs. Shapiro, if all goes well with the filming, we should be able to wrap in a day, and I can arrange the schedule so that Starshine doesn't have to miss any school —"

"Oh, that's all right," I said, pretending not to see the dirty look my mom gave me.

"So what do you say?"

"Please, Mom?"

She hesitated.

"Please please please please —"

"All right."

"YAY!!"

"Wonderful," Mr. Brintmorgan said. He gave my mom

the time and place. Then he said to me, "Ask for Désirée when you get to the studio, Starshine. She'll find you an outfit in Wardrobe and do your makeup, OK?"

"OK!"

"Great. Well, I'd better get back to *Sweltering Safari*," Mr. Brintmorgan said, and with a wave he walked back to the Conservatory.

I threw my arms around my mom. "Thanks, Mom!"

She smiled. "I think I should have my head examined."

"Let's go tell Daddy," I said, running for my bike.

"He's going to think I'm crazy," she said. "I *am* crazy."

"No, you're not! This is great! TV! Oh, I'm so excited!"

We got our bikes and started down the hill. We rolled effortlessly, not even pedalling, fast, faster, faster. My hair streamed back and my eyes ran tears. Faster faster faster — "I'M GOING TO BE ON T-V-E-E-E-E-E!" I hollered all the way down.

Chapter Three

"Daddy, I'm going to be on television!"

"What?" my dad said.

"In a cat food commercial!"

"What?"

My mom and I explained, interrupting each other every minute.

"Who's Charlie?" my dad said.

"The bird."

"What bird?"

"Forget Charlie, Dad. Oh, I'm going to be on TV!" I skipped around the living room.

Peggy came running in. "Me, too?" Her favourite question.

"Nope! Just me."

"I wanna be on TV, too!"

My mom pulled Peggy toward her. "This is just for big girls, Pumpkin."

Peggy's lower lip started trembling. Her cheeks got red. She was revving up for a major tantrum. "I WANNA BE

ON TV!'"

"Peggy —"

She flung herself on the floor and buried her face in the rug, kicking her feet and lifting her head every so often to shout, "I wanna! I wanna! I wanna!"

Finally my dad lifted her by the arms. "I'm sorry, Pumpkin, you can't. But maybe you can go and watch Star make the commercial."

The tears stopped, though she still sniffled.

"That's a good idea. What do you say, Star?" my mom said, giving me a pleading look.

Shoot! I didn't want her there. For once, I was going to be the centre of attention — me, Starshine, instead of my cute, adorable, show-off little sister — and I wanted it all to myself. I didn't want to share it with her. But I knew that if I didn't say yes, it would be tantrum city in our house for days. "Oh, OK," I grumbled.

Peggy wiped her runny nose with her sleeve. She heaved a sigh, as if *she* were the one making the sacrifice.

Oh, well, I told myself, she'll just be watching. She'll be on the sideline. I'll still be the star of the show. Starshine the Star!

Then I ran to the phone and called Julie.

"You what!" she screamed.

"I just happened to be in the right place at the right time," I said modestly, even though I was sure I must have been oozing talent for Mr. Brintmorgan to have spotted me.

"Tell me all about it," Julie said. "What did he say? What

did you say?"

I told her. Then Julie said, "What are you going to wear? Did he tell you?"

"No, he said they'd fix me up when I got to the studio."

"Oh, can you imagine! They probably have racks and racks of costumes."

"I hope it's something cool, like leggings and a T-shirt."

"Or jeans and a matching denim jacket," Julie suggested.

"Yeah ... I wonder what they'll do with my hair."

"Probably fluff it out and curl it more."

"And they'll probably put makeup on me, too. Eye shadow ... lipstick ... blush ..." I imagined myself with my hair done, my face made up. I'd look cool and grown-up, instead of like a skinny, plain almost-eleven-year-old.

"Oh, you lucky duck! I could kill you!" Julie said, laughing. I knew she was jealous — how could she not be? — but happy for me, too. 'Cause she's a real friend.

"Julie," I said, "once I get to know Mr. Brintmorgan better — you know, after I've done a few commercials — I'll ask him if he has anything for you."

"Oh, would you?" Julie gasped.

"I promise."

The next day I told everybody at school. Ms. Hamilton, the school secretary, said, "Congratulations, Starshine!" Mr. Ramu, the custodian, said, "You will be a famous girl!" Ms. Fung, my teacher, said, "How exciting for you, Starshine! You'll have to tell us what it's like being inside a television studio." All the kids said it was cool and I was so lucky and could I bring back autographs if I met anybody famous. Even Jimmy Tyler and Tommy Scott, who always chase Julie and me and tease us, stopped pulling my hair for a couple of days.

I felt like a star already.

TALENT TRAIL STUDIOS, flashed a neon sign. I gave my name to a receptionist. She looked in an appointment book and smiled. "Yes, Starshine, Mr. Brintmorgan is expecting you."

"I'm Peggy," Peggy announced.

"Hello there," the receptionist said. "Aren't you cute?"

Peggy gave her precious grin. "Yup."

The receptionist giggled.

"I'm four," Peggy said, holding up four fingers as if that were a brilliant feat.

"Well, look at that, you can count!" the receptionist said.

"I can spell my name, too," Peggy said. "It's P, E, "

I shoved in front of her. "I'm supposed to ask for Désirée."

"Oh, yes, I'll page her," the receptionist said. She punched some buttons on her phone, spoke into a mouthpiece, and a minute later a woman came walking toward us. She had thick black makeup around her eyes and purple lipstick. Her blonde hair stuck straight up in the air. Her name tag said MAKEUP DEPARTMENT.

"Starshine Shapiro?" she said, looking from me to Peggy.

"That's me," I said quickly.

"Hi. I'm Désirée. Follow me to Wardrobe. We'll pick you an outfit and make you up for the shoot."

I grinned at my mom. Wardrobe! The shoot! Real TV talk.

Désirée led us down a long hallway. The walls were lined with pictures of people who had been discovered by Talent Trail Studios. There was a boy who'd modelled boxer shorts, and a woman who'd done an ad for pimple cream. We paused by a photo of twin babies. "The Fletcher twins," Désirée said. "Aren't they cute?" I nodded. "They did the Bums Diapers commercial. It was really a shame when they got toilet trained."

Then we came to a picture of a girl whom I recognized from *Family Frolics*, a popular TV show. She'd written on her picture, "Dear Mr. B, Thanks for giving me my start. Love, Becky."

Désirée noticed where I was looking. "That's Rebecca Rayside," she said. "She started out doing Friendly's Fish Food commercials. That got her an audition for *Family Frolics*, and it's been stardom all the way."

Wow! I thought. From fish food to a TV series. Maybe it could happen to me. From Kitten Krunchies to ... to ... a major motion picture!

Finally we came to a room marked WARDROBE. "Come on in, honey, let's find you something to wear," Désirée said.

I stepped inside. Holy cow. Every kind of clothes I could possibly imagine was in that room. Clown suits. Tuxedos. Ball gowns. Motorcycle jackets. Baseball caps, chefs' hats, police caps and Davy Crockett raccoon hats. Army boots. High heels. Ballet slippers. High-tops. Could I have a ball in there on Hallowe'en!

I spotted a cool tie-dyed vest. That would look good, I

thought, and looked around for some jeans to match.

Désirée pulled a dress off the rack. It was pink with puffy sleeves, ruffles down the front, a full skirt with lace on the bottom, and a big sash that tied at the back. She held it up against me.

Oh no, I thought.

"Perfect," Désirée said.

Fifteen minutes later I came out in the pink dress, white lacy anklets, black patent leather shoes and a big pink bow on top of my head. This wasn't exactly the cool, grown-up image I'd been hoping for. I looked in the mirror as Désirée tied the sash. Instead of looking sixteen, I looked six.

Oh well, I thought, it's still television. This is just my first break. Things'll be different when I get my own show.

Désirée brushed powder on my face, smeared rouge on my cheeks and rubbed a tiny bit of lipstick on my lips. She stepped back and looked at me. "Precious!"

We went to the studio. There was a kitchen with cupboards and a window and a sink, only it was just the front of a kitchen, like scenery in a play. It looked real, though. On the floor there was a bowl of cat food, covered with plastic wrap, and a giant-sized box of Kitten Krunchies. There were two big cameras on platforms, and bright lights beaming down on the kitchen. Someone was saying "Testing, testing" into a microphone. The camera people were swivelling their cameras and everybody was talking at once.

Mr. Brintmorgan was talking to a man up on a ladder.

After a minute he came over to me, clipboard tucked under his arm. "Starshine, you look marvelous," he said. He turned to my mom. "Didn't I tell you she had it, Mrs. Shapiro?"

My mom agreed that he had.

"I'm Peggy," Peggy said.

"Well, hello there, are you Starshine's little sister?"

"Yup, and I wanted to be on TV too but Mommy said no and then I cried."

"You did?" Mr. Brintmorgan said, bending down to chuck her under the chin. "Well, we don't want any tears around here. We'll just have to see if we can come up with a little surprise to make you feel better, OK?"

"OK." Peggy grinned.

Ugh. Luckily my mom took her away, to some chairs at the side of the set.

I looked around. "Where's the cat?" I asked Mr. Brintmorgan.

"She'll be out in a minute," Mr. Brintmorgan said. "First I want to go through the scene with you and show you the pacing. Now, you stand right here, behind the cat food bowl. That's it. First there's some music, and then the announcer says, 'Kitten Krunchies is the right food for your cat. It's got all the nutrition cats need to make them frisky and healthy, from cuddly little kittens to sleek grown-up cats. Just like Poopsie.'"

"Poopsie?"

"The cat. Now, up until this point, the camera has been on Poopsie. She's eating the Kitten Krunchies. Now the camera zooms in on you, and you smile and say —" He handed me his clipboard.

I read aloud, "I wouldn't feed Poopsie anything but Kitten Krunchies, 'cause that's what she loves best. Right, Poopsie?"

"That's it, very good. Now, when you say 'Right, Poopsie,' you kneel down and pet Poopsie, and the camera pans out as the announcer says, 'Kitten Krunchies. Turkey, oyster and liver flavours.' Then the music comes back on, and that's it. Got it?"

"Uh — sure."

"Good. Let's run through it a few times."

We ran through it, and everything went fine. It didn't take me long to learn my lines. I mean, it wasn't much of a speech. I'd been expecting to have more to say. But Mr. Brintmorgan was happy. He called for someone to bring the cat in. "I'll give you and Poopsie a few minutes to get acquainted, and then we'll do the first take," he said.

A woman with red hair piled high on top of her head came out carrying a Siamese cat. She introduced herself as Arabella and said she was Poopsie's trainer. Poopsie was beautiful. She was white with just a tinge of grey on her coat, and grey paws and a grey tail and blue eyes. She looked right at me, and black slits formed in her eyes. I realized I didn't know very much about cats. What did the black slits mean? Were they friendly or unfriendly? She didn't attack me, so I guessed they were friendly.

I patted Poopsie on the head. "Hi, Poopsie," I said.

"Why don't you hold her on your lap for a while?" Arabella said.

I sat down and she put Poopsie on my lap. I started stroking her. Gosh, she was soft. Long white hairs came off in my fingers and floated around like snowflakes. Poopsie started purring. She sounded like an electric train. "She really likes you. Don't you, Poops?" Arabella said, bending down to Poopsie's face. Poopsie purred louder.

I felt a tickle in my nose, as if I had a speck of dust in it. I wiggled my nose. It still tickled. I sneezed — *achoo!* — all over Poopsie. Poopsie jumped off my lap and ran straight to Arabella.

"Don't sneeze on Poopsie!" Arabella said.

"Sorry, I didn't mean to."

Arabella took a brush out of her pocket and brushed Poopsie's hair. Mr. Brintmorgan came over and said, "Ready?"

"Sure," I said. My nose felt runny. I sniffed loudly, hoping there weren't any drips.

Désirée darted forward, went over my face with a powder brush and lifted up my hair with a thing that looked like an oversized fork.

"All right, places, everyone," Mr. Brintmorgan announced. I got into position and Poopsie crouched at my feet. Someone took the plastic wrap off the bowl of Kitten Krunchies and Poopsie started crunching away. My mom and Peggy waved at me. I grinned back. This was happening! I was really doing it!

Someone said, "Kitten Krunchies, take one."

"Cue the music," Mr. Brintmorgan said. "Ready ... and ... go."

The music started. The announcer started talking about Kitten Krunchies. I smiled. My nose itched again. I really must have gotten dust in it. I kept my face plastered in a smile while I tried to wiggle my nose without moving it. And now it was my turn — "I wouldn't feed Poopsie anything but Kitten Krunchies, 'cause that's what she — *ah-ah-achoo!*"

Poopsie jumped and ran straight for Arabella.

"Cut!" someone yelled.

"Sorry," I said, wiping my nose with my hand.

"That's all right, Starshine," Mr. Brintmorgan said. "Désirée will fix you up." Désirée wiped my nose with a tissue and repowdered my face. By now I felt like my face was a powder mask.

"All right now?" Mr. Brintmorgan said.

I nodded. My nose still felt tickly and my eyes were a little bit itchy. But I was all right. I knew my lines and I was ready.

"Kitten Krunchies, take two."

"Roll the music — ready — and — now."

Music. Announcer. "I wouldn't feed Poopsie anything but Kitten Krunchies 'cause that's what she loves best." I knelt down. "Ri-i-i — *achoo!*"

Poopsie took off.

"Cut!"

My nose was running into my mouth. I was afraid to look up. "Starshine, you didn't tell me you had a cold,"

Mr. Brintmorgan said. He sounded annoyed.

"I don't!" I blew my nose into a tissue Désirée gave me, and wiped my eyes, which were watering a little.

My mom hurried over and felt my forehead. "Do you feel all right, Star?"

"Fine, fine," I said, pushing away her hand. "Just let me wipe my nose." I didn't actually feel fine. My nose tickled, my eyes itched and my chest felt wheezy. But I didn't want anyone to know that.

"Kitten Krunchies is a very important client," Mr. Brintmorgan said, pacing back and forth. "If you're not up to it, we can —"

"Please, Mr. Brintmorgan," I said, "it was just a little sneezing fit. I'm OK now."

Mr. Brintmorgan looked at me doubtfully. "OK," he said. He turned to Arabella. "Is Poopsie all right?"

Arabella nodded, though she gave me a dirty look.

"OK. Places. Quiet, please."

"Kitten Krunchies, take three."

I gritted my teeth into a smile and tried to ignore the itching in my nose, throat and eyes. "I wouldn't feed Poopsie anything but Kitten Krunchies, 'cause that's what she loves. Right, Poo-poo-poo — *achoo! Achoo! Achoo!*"

"Cut!"

Poopsie jumped, knocking over the bowl. Kitten Krunchies spilled on the floor.

"Star, what's wrong?" my mom said, running over to me. "Mr. Brintmorgan, I swear she was fine when we came. Absolutely healthy. No sign of a stuffed nose or anything."

"*Achoo!*"

"Well, if she was so healthy, I'd like to know what would bring on a sneezing fit all of a sudden, unless —" He stopped short. He, my mom, Arabella and Désirée all exchanged looks. "— she's allergic to cats!" they all said at once.

"No!" I wailed. "*Achoo!*"

"I had no idea," my mom said.

"I can't be!" I yelled. "*Achoo — choo — choo!*"

"I'm terribly sorry, Mr. Brintmorgan," my mom said. "Really, we didn't know. She was never around cats —"

"No! I want to be on TV!" I started crying and dripping all over the pink dress.

"It's not your fault, Mrs. Shapiro," Mr. Brintmorgan said. He started pacing again. "But what am I going to do now? The president of Kitten Krunchies is flying in tonight and he expects to see a tape."

He paced. I sniffled. My mom wiped my nose. Everybody in the studio was quiet. Except Peggy. She had Poopsie on her lap and she was crooning, "Nice kitty, nice kitty, such a pretty Poopsie. Nice Poopsie. I wouldn't feed Poopsie anything but Kitten Krunchies, 'cause that's what she loves best. Right, Poopsie?"

Everybody turned and looked at her. She was hunched over Poopsie, petting her, stroking her, practically rubbing her face in Poopsie's fur. There wasn't a sniffle in sight.

Mr. Brintmorgan exchanged looks with my mom. "What did you say, Peggy? Let's hear that again."

Peggy rattled off the line — *my* line — as if she'd been

rehearsing it for hours. When she got to "Right, Poopsie?" Poopsie looked up at her and purred.

Mr. Brintmorgan grinned. "Hallelujah!"

I sneezed.

Désirée took Peggy by the hand and marched her off to WARDROBE — and straight into my part as the Kitten Krunchies Girl.

Chapter Four

I dawdled on the way to school, hoping the bell would ring before anybody saw me. I couldn't face them. What would I say? It was bad enough that I couldn't do the commercial, but that I'd boasted and bragged and made such a big deal out of it was ten times worse. How could I ever live it down?

I tied my shoes ten times. I counted the buds on the rose bush on the corner. (Seventeen.) I rearranged my homework in my pack. The schoolyard came into sight. Ring, bell, ring! I walked slower and slower, till I was moving in slow motion. If I could only delay until the bell rang, I would escape until recess, and then I could hide in the washroom …

"There's Starshine!"

Everybody came running.

"Starshine, how did it go?"

"Were you scared?"

"Did you meet any stars?"

"Can I have your autograph?"

I wanted to hide, put a bag over my head — anything but stand there and talk to them. "I'm not ... I didn't ... I couldn't ..." I swallowed. "I'm allergic."

"What?"

"Allergic?"

"To cats?"

"You didn't do the commercial?"

This was too much for Tommy and Jimmy. They started jumping around. "Achoo! Cough! Cough! Sniff! Sniff! Achoo! Get that cat away from me! Achoooo!"

I turned away, tears stinging my eyes. Just then Julie arrived. She linked her arm through mine. I'd told her the night before. She'd been great. Sympathetic without smothering — a real friend. Now she pulled me away, saying, "Come on, Star, don't pay attention to them."

I fought back the tears. At least I wouldn't give Jimmy and Tommy the satisfaction of seeing me cry. Those jerks, how dare they — but no, *I* was the jerk. I was the one who'd built everything up, showed off like I was such hot stuff. And now I looked like a fool.

All day long I had to explain over and over. Ms. Hamilton said, "Oh, dear, what a shame. I was so looking forward to seeing you on TV."

Not as much as I was.

Mr. Ramu said, "You will not be a famous girl?"

No, but my sister will.

Ms. Fung said, "I'm so sorry it didn't work out, Starshine. Perhaps you'd like to tell us what it was like in the television studio anyway?"

No, I would not. What I would like to do was throw myself down and scream and pound my fists on the ground and have a real-live tantrum — like Peggy.

Peggy, Peggy, Peggy! Ever since she was born, she's been stealing the show. There's just something about her that's so — so — CUTE! No one can resist her, with her chubby cheeks and reddish hair that sticks straight up and her little bump of a nose. And let me tell you, she makes the most of it. She makes funny faces. She talks baby talk. She does little dances and pretends to fall down. And everybody says, "How adorable! What a character! How clever!"

Meanwhile, there I am, not adorable, not a character, not noticed. "Hello, Starshine," people say, patting me on the head, then go straight to Peggy. "Hi there, you little cutie-wootie! How's our little pumpkin? Still as adorable as ever?" No, not *as* adorable, *more* adorable. Without even trying, Peggy's like a magnet for everybody's attention. She pulls it in, right past me.

It's even like that with my grandma when she comes to visit. Last year she stayed with us when my mom and dad went on vacation. I was so good I practically killed myself. I put away the dishes and made my bed and put all the newspapers in the recycling bag, and Grandma didn't say a word. Then Peggy picked up one teeny scrap of paper. She carried it like a trophy to the garbage and Grandma exclaimed, "Just wait till I tell Mommy and Daddy what a wonderful little helper you were, Pumpkin. Won't they be proud?"

And of course they were. "Oh, Pumpkin, what a good girl!" they exclaimed, picking her up and hugging her and kissing her and tickling her, while she giggled and shrieked and I just stood there.

Well, I was sick of it. Sick of Peggy getting all the attention. Sick of her stealing the show. So when Mr. Brintmorgan discovered me, all I could think was, *finally!* Finally I had something that Peggy didn't have. Finally I was noticed. Finally I was in the spotlight instead of her. And then — SHE TOOK IT AWAY!

I was mad. And disappointed. And embarrassed. And jealous. As Julie and I walked away with Jimmy and Tommy's laughter ringing in our ears, I promised myself that I wasn't going to give up. If Peggy could do it, so could I. I'd show her — and everybody else — that I was just as good as she was. *Better.* I'd get on TV some other way. And not just some stupid cat food commercial, either. I'd get on a real show. I didn't care what — a game show, a sit-com, a comedy, a drama, a mystery ... It didn't matter. *I just had to be on TV.*

A few days later I was having milk and bricks in the kitchen with my mom — (Bricks are these health food cookies my dad invented. We call them bricks 'cause they're so hard.) — when there was a knock on the kitchen door. "Yoo-hoo, anybody home?"

"Mrs. Wentworth," my mom said, opening the door. "Come in."

Mrs. Wentworth eased around the door. She had a package in her hands and an excited look on her face. "Hello, Joan. Hello, Starshine. I don't want to interrupt — you're probably in the middle of making dinner —"

"No, no," my mom said. "Actually it's Peter's night to cook. Please, sit down."

Mrs. Wentworth sat down. She's our next-door neighbour and she's really nice. She lets me play with her dog Hughie all the time, and she didn't even get mad that time I threw his ball through her basement window. Mrs. Wentworth is short and round and she always wears pastel-coloured pants, like ice cream flavors. Today they were strawberry-pink.

"I was so excited, I just couldn't wait to show you," she said, opening the package. "My latest spoon!"

She pulled back tissue paper and there, in a plastic case, was a small silver spoon. The bottom of the handle was shaped like a guitar. "Hey, Mrs. Wentworth, I didn't know you were into rock'n'roll," I said.

"Pardon me?"

"It's a violin," my mom said under her breath, poking me with her elbow.

Mrs. Wentworth gave me a confused look. "It's the Seventy-Fifth Anniversary Stradivarius Society Collector's Silver Spoon!" she said.

"Of course," I said.

My mom gave me a look.

Mrs. Wentworth collects little silver spoons and keeps them in a fancy glass cabinet in her living room. She's got about a hundred of them. I know this because she showed them to me once, one at a time. Frankly, I can't see what would make a person collect spoons. I mean, *spoons*? And it's not as though she uses them — they just sit in the cabinet. But she's very proud of her collection, so I always pretend to be interested.

"It's lovely, Mrs. Wentworth," my mom said. "A fine addition to your collection."

"My one-hundred-fifth spoon," Mrs. Wentworth said proudly.

"No kidding!" my mom said.

Mrs. Wentworth put the spoon back in the box. "I hate to say it, though, but this one isn't my favourite. I think my favourite is the Abdominal Association Spoon, with the large intestine engraved on the handle. Or maybe the Royal Reptile Society one, with the bowl shaped like a crocodile. Or perhaps ..."

I said I had homework.

After a little while my mom asked me to walk Mrs. Wentworth home. "Next door?" I started to ask, but then I saw that my mom had an armful of magazines, which she wanted me to carry for Mrs. Wentworth. So I followed her across our yard and then across her yard and then up her back steps and dumped the magazines on the kitchen counter. "Thank you, Starshine," Mrs. Wentworth said. She went to put her new spoon in the glass cabinet. I turned to go and got a faceful of Hughie's tongue.

"Hughie!" I said. "Blech!"

Hughie slunk down. He knows he's not supposed to

jump up on people. But he gets so excited, he forgets. He looked at me, his tail slapping the wall. "Oh, OK, Hughie, go get your ball," I said.

He swished his tail joyously, bounded out of the room and was back in a minute with a soggy, fuzz-less tennis ball, which he dropped at my feet. *Squwudge*, went the ball. I picked it up with my fingertips and carried it outside, Hughie at my heels. I loved Hughie but his ball was gross.

"Go get it, boy," I called.

Hughie got it, drooling and slurping. *Squwudge*.

I threw the ball several more times. Each time I said, "This is the last one, Hughie," but he gave me such a pitiful look that I picked the ball up again, wiping my slimy hands on my jeans.

Finally I said, "This is the last time, Hughie. I mean it." While he ran to fetch the ball, I escaped. Almost. Hughie ambushed me as I was crossing into my yard. Thwump, thwump, went his long black tail.

I didn't look him in the eye. "Hughie — NO."

After dinner that night, my dad and I were sitting at either end of the couch with our legs on top of each other. He was reading the paper and I had a stack of Archie comics. He was whistling "Skip to my Lou." He whistles a lot.

All of a sudden he stopped whistling and said, "Star, don't you know a girl named Chatham?"

"Yeah, Lucy," I said without looking up. "Why?"

"Her house was robbed."

I looked up. "Really?"

"Yeah, the thief took silver. Bowling trophies."

"Bowling trophies?"

"Mmm-hmm. Worth quite a bit, apparently. Says here it was the third burglary in this neighbourhood in the past month."

"Let's see." I untangled my legs from my dad's and looked over his shoulder. BURGLAR BOWLS A STRIKE, said the headline. But my eye was caught by another headline on the page. AUDITIONS, it said in big letters.

"Give me that!" I said, snatching the newspaper out of my dad's hands.

"Hey!"

I ignored him and read:

AUDITIONS
Munchkins are needed for a television special
of *The Wizard of Oz*. Boys and girls, aged 8-12,
up to 5 feet in height.
Saturday, April 24, 9:00-2:00
False Creek Community Centre.
Bring résumé. Be prepared to sing and dance
"Follow the Yellow Brick Road."

"Dad, how tall am I?" I asked anxiously.

"Gee, I don't know, four-eight, four-nine?"

"Whew!"

"What? Why? Can I have my paper back?"

"Sure." I handed it to him. Here was my chance to get on TV! A Munchkin in *The Wizard of Oz*! And boy, was that ten times better than being the Kitten Krunchies girl, or what?

The phone rang. "Hello?"

"Star, did you see the paper?" It was Julie.

"What, about Lucy?"

"Lucy who?"

"Lucy Chatham."

"No, silly, the auditions!"

"Oh, yeah, I did."

"Are you going?"

"Yeah, are you?"

"YEAH!"

I jerked the phone away from my ear. "Julie, don't yell."

"Sorry. Oh, Star, I'm so excited!"

"Me, too."

"*The Wizard of Oz*!"

"Television!"

"Want to go to the audition together?" Julie said.

"Sure."

"I'm sure we'll both get in, aren't you?"

I didn't answer right away. I was sure *I'd* get in — after all, I had presence. Mr. Brintmorgan had said so. And if it hadn't been for that stupid allergy, I'd have been a TV star already. But Julie — well, I didn't know. Not that she wasn't good, but did she have that certain something? But I didn't want to hurt her feelings, so I said, "Sure we will."

"OH, STAR!"

"Julie!"

"Sorry." She giggled. I heard her mom call her. "Oops, gotta go. See you, Star."

"'Bye."

As soon as I hung up, I hunted through our stack of videotapes, found *The Wizard of Oz* and popped it into the VCR. I fast-forwarded to the part where the Munchkins sing "Follow the Yellow Brick Road" and played it again … and again … and again …

Finally my dad said, "Starshine, if I hear that blasted song one more time, I'm going to feed the tape to Hughie."

Hughie would eat it, too. But I didn't need the sound anymore — I'd memorized the words. Now I just had to learn the dance. So I put the tape on mute and started copying the steps. Or tried to. It wasn't as easy as it looked. When the Munchkins did their little skippety-hop, I got my feet tangled up and fell down. I picked myself up, ignoring my dad's chuckle from behind the newspaper, and studied the Munchkins again. Foot out, big step, little step with the other foot, hop on it at the same time — yikes! — CRASH!

"Darn," I said, rewinding.

Maybe if I sang while I did the steps. "We're off" — step on right, catch up with left, right again — "OW!" I'd stepped on my own foot.

Rewind.

"We're off" — step right, hop left, step right, YES! — "to see the Wizard" — step left, step right, now what? cross with left — I was facing backwards.

"DARN!"

"What is it, Star?" my mom asked, coming into the living room.

"She's going to be a Munchkin," my dad said.

"Me, too," Peggy said, following my mom in. "What's a Munchkin?"

"A Munchkin?" my mom said. Then she saw the TV. The Munchkins were silently dancing and singing their way down the Yellow Brick Road. My mom's eyes filled with tears. She always cries over *The Wizard of Oz*. When Dorothy says goodbye to the wizard, Mom's a basket case.

I showed my mom the newspaper. "Can I go?"

"Sure."

"I wanna be a Munchkin!" Peggy shouted.

"You can't," I told her. "You have to be eight." Hah! Peggy couldn't steal this one from me, even if she wanted to.

And besides, she already had enough glory. More than enough. She went around in a Kitten Krunchies T-shirt, drank her milk from a Kitten Krunchies mug and carried her preschool snack in a Kitten Krunchies backpack, all sent to her by Mr. Brintmorgan.

Strangers recognized her in the grocery store. "Isn't that the adorable little girl in the cat food commercial?" I heard people whisper as we stood in the checkout line.

Our neighbour, Mr. Hooper, always made a point of stopping us as we walked by. "And how's our little Kitten Krunchies Girl today?" he'd ask. "Oh, hello, Starshine."

Even my mom and dad got into the act. Every time Peggy's smiling face came on TV, they clustered around the set and said, "Oh, Pumpkin, you did such a good job! We're so proud of you!"

Well, enough was enough. It was my turn now. All I had to do was practise and practise, and I'd be a Munchkin. *Then* I'd get a piece of that spotlight Peggy was hogging.

Chapter Five

In front of Julie and me as far as we could see, and behind us as far as we could see, kids filled the False Creek Community Centre. Some had their parents hovering over them, some were on their own. Some were with friends, others were alone. Some wiggled and jittered, some stood perfectly still except to shuffle forward as the line moved up. From all around us came voices singing "Follow the Yellow Brick Road" — in a dozen different keys. It sounded like an orchestra tuning up.

Julie was number 71 and I was number 72. Number 70, the boy in front of Julie, kept singing up the scale, do-re-mi-fa-sol-la-ti-do, and down again, do-ti-la-sol-fa-mi-re-do. Up and down, up and down. Every time he hit "la" he was flat. I was sure he didn't have a chance.

Number 73, the girl behind me, was singing "Follow the Yellow Brick Road" in an annoying squeaky Munchkin voice. She seemed to have the Munchkins mixed up with the Chipmunks. She didn't have a chance, either.

I felt like laughing. I wasn't even nervous! I had a little

flutter in my stomach, but it wasn't a scared kind of flutter, just an excited one. I felt good. I knew the words. I knew the steps. Mr. Brintmorgan said I had presence. What did I have to worry about? Nothing. I was ready to show them my stuff and find out when to show up for rehearsals.

Julie, on the other hand, was a wreck. First she'd bite her nails. Then she'd tuck her hair behind her ears. Then she'd crack her knuckles. Bite, tuck, crack. Finally she turned and said, "Star, I'm going to throw up."

I backed up a step, nearly stomping on Number 73. "Not on me!"

"No, not really," Julie said. "I couldn't, I don't have anything in me to bring up. You know why? 'Cause I didn't eat any breakfast. Couldn't. Did you eat breakfast? My mom told me I should eat, but I couldn't. I tried. Cheerios. With banana. I just couldn't get it down. I ate one bite and quit. I had butterflies. Did you eat, Star? I knew I should try to eat but I just —"

I put my fingers around her neck and pretended to squeeze.

"OK, OK, I get it," she said with a nervous laugh. "Did you eat breakfast?"

"Sure."

"What did you have?'

"Granola."

"How could you eat? I couldn't eat a bite —"

"Julie," I warned.

"Oops," she said with a guilty smile.

We moved forward.

"I wonder how long the auditions take," Julie said.

"Well, we seem to be moving every few minutes," I said.

"Just a few minutes! What if you blow it? Do they give you a second chance?"

"I don't know." I wasn't going to blow it, that was for sure. I knew the song and dance cold.

"I wonder if they tell you right away whether you made it," Julie said, her forehead puckered.

Before I had a chance to answer, she went on, "But how could they? They have to hear everybody first. It wouldn't be fair to say yes to some people without hearing everybody, would it? But then we won't know! We'll have to wait. Oh, Star, I can't wait. I'll die!"

"You'll die if you say another word," I warned her.

She giggled nervously.

Do-re-mi-fa-sol-laaaa-ti-do, sang Number 70, as flat as ever. Julie and I moved up as one by one, kids came out of the audition room. Some were smiling, others looked grim. I imagined how impressed the judges would be when I told them I'd nearly been in a Kitten Krunchies commercial. "My, you must be talented!" I pictured them saying as they shook my hand.

We edged around a corner. Now we could see the door of the audition room and hear the piano. We were about five kids from the front. Julie started bouncing up and down. "Oh, Star, I'm so excited!" she said. Bounce-bounce-bounce. "I can't stand it!" Bounce-bounce-bounce. "I'm going to burst!" Bounce-bounce-bounce.

"Julie, stop bouncing."

"Am I bouncing?"

"Yes, and you're making me seasick."

"Oh, sorry." She kept still for about a minute. Bounce-bounce-bounce —

"Julie!"

"Sorry!"

With a final do-re-mi, the kid in front of Julie went in. We listened at the door. There was some talking, then the piano started. You could barely hear the boy singing over the piano. More talking, then silence, then talking. The door opened. He stared at the floor.

"How was it?" someone said.

He just scowled. Julie gave me a terrified look.

"Number 71," a voice called.

Julie jumped.

"Break a leg," I whispered.

She went in. There was some talking. Then the piano started playing. I could hear Julie's voice, clear and pretty. There was more talking, then laughter. The door opened. Julie came out with a huge grin on her face. "It was great! They're so nice! They said I'd probably get a callback."

Wow!

"Number 72."

All of a sudden I got scared. All this time I hadn't been the slightest bit nervous. I'd been relaxed. I'd been coasting along, waiting for my turn. Now it was my turn — and I was terrified. Panicked. Scared to death. I couldn't go in there and sing and dance in front of a bunch of strangers!

"Break a leg, Star," Julie whispered.

You know how in fairy tales the wicked witch casts a spell on the good princess and turns her into stone? That's how I felt. Frozen.

"Number 72?"

Forcing myself to put one foot in front of the other, I marched into the audition room. There was a piano at one end where a woman with curly grey hair was leaning on one elbow, looking bored, and a table at the other end where two women and a man were sitting. One of the women had short blonde hair and bright red lips. She had just put on fresh lipstick and was looking at herself in a little mirror. The other woman had long black hair and black eye makeup and black fingernail polish and she was dressed all in black. The man had a curly brown beard, like my dad. I noticed that there were two piles of paper on the table, one thick and the other thin.

"Number 72?" the blonde woman said, snapping her mirror shut.

I jumped. "Y-yes," I said, my voice cracking. My throat was so dry I could hardly swallow.

"Hi, there," the woman in black said with a smile. The others just sat there. They didn't smile. Julie had said they were really nice, but those two weren't being nice to me.

The blonde woman said, "Your résumé, please."

"What?"

"Your résumé?"

I looked at my hand and realized I was still holding my résumé. "Oh, yeah." As I handed it to her, I dropped it on the floor. "Whoops." Then I stepped on it. Now my résumé had a shoeprint on it. Great. I tried to brush off the dirt and got the paper all wrinkled. Finally I shoved it into her hand. It said:

STARSHINE BLISS SHAPIRO
Height: 4 feet, 8 1/2 inches
Age: 10 3/4
<u>Theatrical Experience</u>
"The Story of Arachne," an original play by
Starshine Shapiro and Julie Wong. Won first
prize for grade four at Priscilla Marpole
Elementary School in the Charlotte Feldenstock
Memorial "The Myths Come Alive" contest.
(I was Arachne.)

She glanced over it in about two seconds and said, "No television? No professional work?"

"Well, almost," I said, giving what I hoped was a bright smile. "You see, I was supposed to be in a Kitten Krunchies commercial, but I turned out to be allergic to cats." I paused, waiting for sympathy. No one said anything. "My little sister got the part," I added.

"That cute little Kitten Krunchies girl is your sister?" the man said.

I nodded.

"She's adorable! What presence!"

I wanted to scream.

The woman in black said, "OK, Starshine, now we'd like

to hear you sing and dance. Mrs. Potwick will play a little intro and then you come in. OK?" Even though she looked ghastly, she had a friendly voice.

"OK."

The piano player — Mrs. Potwick — started playing "We're off to see the Wizard, the wonderful Wizard of Oz." When she came to "Oz," she held the note, so I knew it was my cue to come in. I opened my mouth. Nothing came out. I couldn't think of the words. I was blank.

The music stopped. The man said, as if he were talking to a two-year-old, "Follow the yellow brick road — remember?"

Tears flooded my eyes. I felt so stupid. And I hated that man. He didn't have to be so snotty about it.

"I'm sorry," I said, clapping my hand to my forehead. "I don't know what happened —"

"That's all right," the lady in black said kindly. "It was just stage fright. Start again."

I took a deep breath, swallowing down the tears. Mrs. Potwick played the intro. I came in on cue. "Follow the Yellow Brick Road. Follow the Yellow Brick Road. Follow, follow, follow, follow, follow the Yellow Brick Road. We're OFF —" I took a large leap and banged into a chair, which fell over with a clatter. "The wonderful Wizard of Oz —" My voice sounded weak against the loud thumping of the piano. "We hear he is a whiz of a wiz —" I took an extra hop and got my feet crossed up. "If ever a wiz there was —" I stomped on my own foot. "Because, because, because, because, BECAUSE —" I was shrieking. The blonde woman covered her ears. "The wonderful Wizard of Oz!" I finished with my arms raised — and my back to the judges. Quickly, I whirled around, trying to make it look like part of the dance.

There was a moment of silence. The blonde woman removed her hands from her ears. The three of them whispered together. The man said, "That'll be all, number 72. Thank you for trying out."

I stood there. There had to be a mistake. They didn't understand — I had to get picked!

"But —" I began.

"I know it's disappointing," said the woman in black kindly. "So many children audition and we can only take twelve."

I glanced at my résumé, now lying on top of the big pile. The rejects. She followed my glance. "I'm sure you're quite good at acting. Maybe singing and dancing just isn't your thing." She smiled.

I walked out in a daze. I wanted to blame it on them, to say that they'd been unfair, that they hadn't given me a chance. But the truth was, I'd stunk. I knew I had. And now I'd blown my chance to be on TV and show that I was as good as Peggy. Everything was ruined. I just wanted to find a quiet corner and howl. Instead I walked straight into Julie's great big smile.

"Well?" she said, grabbing my arm. "Well?"

I didn't answer.

"You didn't make it?" She sounded truly shocked. I shook my head. "Oh, Star!"

"I knocked over a chair."

"I wondered what that noise was."

"It was me being a klutz."

"Oh, Star." Julie's voice was full of sympathy.

I didn't want her sympathy. "Well, at least *you* made it," I said.

"Hey, wait a minute, I'm not in yet."

"You will be." Of course she would. She could sing. She could dance. She had talent.

"Just because I got a callback doesn't mean I'm automatically in," Julie argued. "There's probably tons of kids better than me."

I was on the verge of crying. "Oh, come off it, Julie. You're good and I'm not —"

"Star —"

"— and you know it —"

"Star —"

"— so you can stop pretending to be so — so — darn *modest,* right this minute." I stomped away, leaving her standing there in the hallway.

When I got home, it was time to test Goldy-legs's web. I wasn't in the mood for it. I wasn't in the mood for anything except climbing in bed, pulling the covers over my head, and pretending I'd never heard of *The Wizard of Oz.*

But I had to do the weighing. This was an important scientific experiment, after all, and I had to follow the proper procedure. I got the weighing posts ready, unfolded the RECORD OF WEB STRENGTH, and sharpened my pencil. Then I teased Goldy-legs out of the web and carefully lifted it from the porch wall.

This week I was feeding her flies. Since I'd tried a hard-shelled insect the first week, I'd decided to try a soft-bodied insect this week. Fred had agreed. He said that was excellent scientific thinking. He said I was varying the variables. I wasn't sure what that meant, but I was pretty sure it was good.

I stretched the web over the weighing posts. It looked better than last week's, I thought. A little thicker. A little stronger. A little tighter. Or was that only wishful thinking?

One golf ball ... two golf balls ... four ... five ... HOLY COW! Seven ... HOLD! HOLD! ... eight golf — Rrrrip! Clunkety — clunk-clunk.

But, still, look at that! Seven golf balls, times fifty grams, came to ... three hundred and fifty grams! Wow! That sure was better than last week. We were making progress.

"Way to go, Goldy-legs!" I said. My voice sounded lonely, cheering all by itself. I wished Julie were there to cheer with me.

Chapter Six

Julie didn't call to tell me she got the part. I only found out when Lucy Chatham said to me at school a few days later, "Isn't it great about Julie?"

So I knew. And it hurt. I was jealous. I hated being jealous, but I was. And embarrassed, 'cause I did so bad. But most of all, I was mad — at myself, really — for blowing it.

Ms. Fung called Julie to the front of the class and said she was "our budding thespian," whatever that was. The other kids flocked around her, shared their snacks with her, whispered secrets to her. At recess Miranda Stockton let her go first at skipping rope instead of having to stand in line like everyone else. Jimmy and Tommy called her "Munchie," and they tried to make it sound teasing, but even they couldn't keep the admiration out of their voices.

Not that Julie showed off. I'll give her that. Some kids would have used every excuse to drop the director's name or talk about rehearsals or make it sound like they were best buddies with Dorothy. Julie didn't do that. She didn't talk about the show unless somebody else brought it up. When people told her how cool she was, she looked uncomfortable, like she wished they'd stop. When everybody started crowding around her at recess, saying, "Julie, want to play catch? Julie, want one of my cookies?" she looked around until she caught my eye, and she seemed to be asking me to come to her. But she didn't say anything, and neither did I, and then she'd get caught up by the others, swept away in the middle of a giggling crowd. I let her. I wasn't going to make a big deal out of her. I wasn't going to butter her up. If she wanted to hang out with kids who just wanted to be with her because she'd gotten on a TV show, then that was her business.

One day our class played floor hockey in gym, girls against boys. Everybody ran around, chasing the puck up and down the gym floor. The boys faked the girls out, the girls passed around the boys, the boys bragged about how they were going to whip the wimpy girls, the girls laughed about the stupid macho boys. With the game all tied up I beat Tommy to the puck and passed through a crowd of boys' legs to a team-mate (who turned out to be Julie, though I didn't know it at the time), who shot in the winning goal past Jimmy. Then all the girls whooped and hollered and told the stunned boys that they'd better stick to playing the kindergarteners from now on.

We trooped into the girls' change room, laughing and cheering as we changed out of our gym clothes. "Females rule!" Lucy Chatham yelled.

"Did you see the look on Jimmy's face when the puck went in?" Sharon Giannone said, and she made a face of disbelief. Everybody laughed.

"We kicked butt!" Miranda shouted and everybody said, "Miranda!" She didn't usually talk that way. But Miranda just blushed and laughed.

One by one the girls got changed and left, and before I knew it, Julie and I were the only ones left. An awkward silence fell. We took off our shorts. We put on our clothes. We did up our shoes. All without a word. Finally I couldn't stand it anymore. I said stiffly, "How are rehearsals?"

"Fine," Julie said, not looking at me.

"That's nice." I was polite.

"Geez, Star, you could be happy for me!" Julie exploded.

"No, I can't!" That was the truth. I couldn't be happy for my best friend and it felt awful. It felt like a rotten thing in my stomach.

"Oh, Star," Julie said, dismayed, "I've tried not to rub it in —"

"Aren't you nice."

"What do you want, Star? I can't help it if I got in and you didn't —"

"— if you're talented and I'm not, you mean. Why don't you just come out and say it?"

"All right then, maybe it's true!" Julie yelled.

That shocked me.

"And maybe it's not!" she added just as angrily. "Maybe I had a good day and you had a bad day. But that's how it goes. I didn't mean for it to turn out this way, but it did.

And — and —" Her voice trembled.

"What?"

"— I can't enjoy it without you. It's not the same."

"Oh, Julie!" I burst out crying. "Oh, Ju-Ju-l-l-lie." I put my arms around her. She started crying too.

The rotten feeling in my stomach started to go away. "I-I w-wanted it so bad," I blubbered into her shoulder.

"I know."

"I felt so awful."

"I know."

"I was so bad."

"Were you really?" Julie asked.

"Really," I said, pulling away and looking at her. "I forgot the words, and then I knocked over a chair, and then I ended up with my back to the judges —" Suddenly it seemed funny, and I burst out laughing. Julie laughed, too, and then I cried some more, and we both laughed again.

"Friends?" Julie said.

"Sure!"

"Good! Oh, Star, there are so many funny little things that I've been dying to tell you — stuff that no one else would think was funny."

"Except me," I said with a grin. I felt the grin spread throughout my body. "Like what?"

"Well," Julie said, wiping her eyes and leaning close, "the kid next to me, Roberto, picks his nose. And eats it."

"Yuck!"

"And then I have to hold his hand."

"YUCK!"

We both laughed.

"And the kid on the other side, Dennis? He wears purple boxers with yellow bunny rabbits on them."

"How do you know?"

"We were trying on costumes."

"You looked?"

"Like you wouldn't?"

"Of course not!" We both laughed.

Just then Miranda ran in. "Oh, here you are! Ms. Fung was wondering what happened to you."

"Oh, gosh," I said.

"Are we in trouble?" Julie said.

"Not our budding thespian," I said, but I said it kindly.

Julie giggled. "What *is* a thespian, anyway?"

"Beats me."

Laughing, we linked arms and followed Miranda down the hall.

That day when I got home from school, my mom and dad were both sitting at the kitchen table, looking at a sheet of paper.

"Multi-media," my dad said.

"Environmental harmony," my mom said.

"Sculptural motifs."

"Earthbound, yet uplifted."

"Skyward. Celestial. Soaring."

"What are you guys talking about?" I said.

"Oh, hi, Star," my dad said, looking up. "It's a contest."

"From the Earthkeepers Society," my mom added.

"The Earth Sings the Sky."

"What?"

"Here." My mom handed me the paper.

> AN ENVIRONMENTAL ART CONTEST
> SPONSORED BY THE EARTHKEEPERS SOCIETY
> OF MOOSE JAW, SASKATCHEWAN.
> CREATE A WORK OF ART FOR OUR NEW
> SOLAR-POWERED HEAD OFFICE.
> YOUR ART WORK MUST REFLECT THE THEME
> "THE EARTH SINGS THE SKY."
> ANY MEDIUM IS ACCEPTABLE.

"Are you guys going to enter?" I said.

"Of course!" my mom said. "We're going to unite clay and stained glass to create a fabulous work of art."

"Cool!" I said. "What'll it be?" I asked.

"That's what we're trying to figure out," my dad said. He grabbed a sketch pad and made some lines with a pencil. "How about something like this, Joanie? A thick jungle, trees and bushes, clouds hanging down, like it's a humid day, you know how sticky it gets in the jungle, and a bolt of lightning — yeah! I can do a great lightning bolt out of blue glass —"

"No, no, Pete," my mom said, grabbing the pad and turning the page. "We've got to get the musical element into it. *Sings the sky.* Music. Voices. Singing rivers. Singing wolves. Singing canaries. Yeah! I can do some clay canaries with musical notes coming out of their mouths, rising to heaven, like this." She sketched away.

My dad shook his head. "Too celestial, Joan. You've got to keep your feet on the ground. Hey, that's it! How about feet — no bodies, just feet — walking on the earth? Like the nameless billions on the planet, toiling and trudging ..."

"Pete, really," my mom said, rolling her eyes. "Feet. Come on. Now, mouths. Yes, there's an idea. Mouths singing, little tongues —"

I left the kitchen as fast as I could.

Over the next few days the house was littered with designs. Sheets of paper were strewn on countertops, piled up in wastebaskets. Every time I looked, my parents were either poring over the sketchbook, their heads together, saying, "Yes, yes, it speaks to me!" or else they were wadding up drawings and throwing them at each other. Then one day they said they'd come up with a design that they both loved — my mom said it was "organic" and my dad said it had "really good vibes."

"Let's see," I said.

They shook their heads. "We want it to be a surprise," my mom said. "We'll show you when it's done."

So for the next week they practically lived in their workshop. They only came out to eat. That was fine with me — I figured all that extra heat from the kiln could only be good for Goldy-legs. Then one day they opened the door and said, "Ta-DA-A-A!"

Peggy and I entered the workshop. There on the table was this — *thing*. It was about three feet high. The bottom part was a turtle made of blue clay, and on its back was an elephant also made of clay, kind of a pukey yellow-green colour. The elephant's head was lifted up and its mouth was open, the trunk rolled back, and out of its mouth came long curvy streams, which I strongly hoped weren't digested peanuts that the elephant was throwing up. The streams, which were made of purple, red, orange and green stained glass, got all tangled up together and turned into a face up at the top — I think it was a woman. Her eyes and mouth were wide open and she looked alarmed. I didn't blame her. Between swirling around in elephant puke and not having a body, who wouldn't be freaked out?

My parents were beaming. "Well?" they said.

"The big elephant is hurting the poor turtle?" Peggy asked.

"No, Pumpkin, it doesn't hurt the turtle one bit," my dad assured her.

"OK," she said, relieved.

They looked at me. Uh-oh. I thought fast. "I love elephants!"

"See, I told you it was a great design," my mom said, giving my dad a big slurpy kiss.

"I knew it all along," he said, kissing her back.

Week Three of the spider experiment, I was feeding Goldy-legs moths. Fluttery, dusty-looking moths. I gagged when I thought of those wings going down her throat, but she didn't seem to mind. She gobbled them up as though they were candy. After I fed her the first one, she wiggled her legs as if to say, "Yum, that was good," and the next day she scooted right over to the edge of the web when I came with the jar. After chowing down, she gave me a look that seemed to say, "What, no more?"

Julie came to help again, and we quickly got the weighing posts and golf balls ready. "Week Three," Julie wrote. "Moths."

I shooed Goldy-legs out of the web, carefully lifted it out of the corner and placed it on the weighing posts.

Julie and I took turns with the golf balls. "Golf ball number one ..." I said.

"Number two ..."

"Number three ..."

"Six ..." I gave Julie a look.

"Seven ..."

The web sagged, stretched, pulled — but held.

"Nine ..." I was hardly breathing now.

"Ten ..." Julie whispered.

"I can't look!" I said, but of course I looked as I placed the eleventh golf ball in. It held.

"T — tw —" R-r-r-rip. Plonkety-clunkety-boink, twelve golf balls bounced to the floor.

"ELEVEN!" I hollered.

"Way to go, Goldy-legs!" Julie said.

We grabbed each other's arms and whirled around. "Eleven! Eleven!"

"Oh, Goldy-legs, I love you!" I yelled.

"Now, that really is going too far," Julie said.
I laughed, whirling until my head spun.

Mr. Brintmorgan called. He said Kitten Krunchies was doing so well — *because of Peggy, of course* — that the company was adding a new product, called Biskittens. They were tiny biscuits in the shape of kittens. Mr. Brintmorgan said the president of Kitten Krunchies, Arthur Molesworth, wanted Peggy for the Biskittens commercial and no one else would do.

"I'm gonna be on TV again?" she said, delighted.

"Yes, Pumpkin, because you were so good the last time," my mom said.

"You're the princess of cat food advertising!" my dad said.

"I'm Princess Peggy," Peggy said.

I didn't go. I couldn't bear to watch. She came back from the studio with her very own jacket. It was made of shiny gold material and on the back, in red letters, it said PEGGY — THE KITTEN KRUNCHIES GIRL. She wore it to bed.

When the Biskittens commercial started appearing on TV, I vowed that if I saw her cute little face smiling out at me one more time I would scream.

A few days later, when I got home from school, my parents were jumping around the kitchen, shrieking.

"What's the matter?" I said, alarmed.

My mom grabbed my dad by the shoulders and they spun around. "Wa-hoooo!!" she yelled.

"What?" I said.

"Oh, Star!" She grabbed me and twirled me so hard I nearly fell over.

"Whoa! What is it?" I said, grabbing a chair for support.

"It's so wonderful!" she hollered.

"First prize!" my dad boomed.

"For what?"

"The contest!" my mom cried. "The Earth Sings the Sky!"

"You mean that — that *thing* actually —" I checked myself. "— I mean, hey, that's great!"

They were too excited to notice. "Moose Jaw, Saskatchewan, here we come!" my mom said, and they started hugging again.

I picked up the letter that was lying on the table. The president of the Earthkeepers Society congratulated them and invited them to come to Moose Jaw to receive their prize at a gala ceremony and watch as their "magnificent work of art was officially installed in the Earthkeepers' office lobby, where it would stand as a lasting monument to environmental harmony."

"Prize?" I said. "What prize?"

"A solar cooker," my dad said, and handed me a flyer. It showed a kind of flat box that was shiny on the back and the sides, and clear in the front and on the top — so the sunshine could get in, I guess. It said the solar cooker was great for cooking tofu hot dogs, and on a sunny day it could boil water in two minutes.

"It always rains here," I observed, but my mom and dad were too busy looking at the calendar to notice.

"Three weeks from tomorrow," my mom said, pointing. "I can't wait!"

"Can Peggy and I come?" I asked. Not that the idea of Moose Jaw was so thrilling, but anything to get out of school.

They shook their heads. "You can't miss school," my mom said.

"And besides, Peggy has another shoot," my dad added.

"I'll call Grandma," my mom said. "I'm sure she'll be glad to come."

Oh great, I thought. Just what I needed.

Grandma was Peggy's biggest fan.

Chapter Seven

A few days later, our class was just getting ready for math when Ms. Fung asked if anybody was familiar with the TV show *Young Einsteins*.

I raised my hand hesitantly, along with a few other kids. I'd heard of the show but never watched it. I knew it was a TV quiz show for kids, on the InfoChannel, which everybody calls the Nerd Network. The InfoChannel carries such fascinating programs as "Inside Cumulus Clouds" and "The Abacus: The First Calculator."

"Well, *Young Einsteins* is looking for new contestants," Ms. Fung said. "Two girls and two boys. The children who are on the show now are getting too old. They're nearly thirteen. So the producers are holding tryouts for kids aged ten to twelve. And I think we have several people in our class who could do very well."

Miranda's hand shot up. "What kind of stuff do you have to know, Ms. Fung?"

Ms. Fung read from a sheet of paper. "Contestants should have a general knowledge of science, history, geography, mathematics and the arts. Also they must be able to respond quickly to questions and have an engaging screen presence."

There was a buzz of conversation.

"Geography — ugh!"

"Quick, what's the capital of Zimbabwe?"

"I stink in science!"

"Is Einstein the guy with the fuzzy hair?"

"Who would want to be on the Nerd Network?"

Me! I thought. But did I? The Nerd Network was for nerds. But still, it *was* TV. A real program. And it might be my only chance to show I was as good as Peggy.

Ms. Fung tapped her desk for quiet. "I've photocopied the information about the tryouts. You may take a slip if you're interested. I encourage all of you to give it a try. At the very least it'll be an interesting experience, and you might even make it. Let's try to get some children from Priscilla Marpole Elementary School on *Young Einsteins*! In your math books please turn to page 86 ..."

All through math I wondered if I should try out. It could be fun to be on *Young Einsteins*, I told myself. But could I make it? I *did* have an engaging screen presence, as long as I didn't have to dance or sing, so I should have a good shot at getting chosen. But was I smart enough? What if I made it and the other contestants turned out to be kids whose idea of fun was to read the dictionary? But maybe I'd get to travel all over Canada — that would be cool. But what if I had to study all the time? What a drag! But maybe I'd get a gold *Young Einsteins* jacket with my name on the back.

Back and forth I went, one minute thinking yes and the next minute thinking no. It was a good thing Ms. Fung didn't call on me. I didn't even know what we were studying.

At recess I waited to see who took slips. Miranda, of course. Dev Chandra. He's a science whiz. He once built a model of the solar system and won first prize in the science fair.

I hesitated. *Young Einsteins* wasn't a commercial that thousands of people would see. It wasn't a famous musical to which everybody knew the words. But it was television. A real show. It was on every week. And — let's face it — it was probably my last chance to get on TV.

I took a slip.

"Borneo," I said.

"Borneo?" my dad repeated.

I looked up from the almanac I was reading. "Yes, Borneo. One of the key products of Borneo is rubber."

"I'm glad you told me that. I was just wondering about the key products of Borneo. Just this minute I was asking myself —"

"Dad." I flipped through the almanac. "Do you know where the highest waterfall in the world is?"

"No. Where is it, honey?"

"Angel Falls, in Venezuela."

"Oh. Remind me not to get inside any barrels the next

time I go to Venezuela."

"Very funny."

My parents were kind of treating the audition as a joke. Well, not a joke exactly, but they couldn't figure out why I wanted to do it. When I'd asked my mom if I could try out, she'd said, "Sure, I guess so. But why?"

"'Cause."

"'Cause why? You know you're smart. Why do you want to go on TV and show you're smarter than a bunch of other kids?"

So I can show Peggy up, I wanted to say. So I can get some attention. 'Cause I've got the TV bug and I'm dying to get my face on the screen. "I just do."

"Star," my dad said anxiously, "have we said anything that made you feel we weren't satisfied with your last report card?"

"No."

"We didn't mind that C+ in math, really."

"I know."

"Well, then?"

"I just have to."

My mom and dad looked at each other. The look said, What's this all about? and, I don't know, and, I think it's OK, and, We'll discuss it later — all in a split second. I know my parents' looks pretty well. After all, I've been living with them for nearly eleven years.

So they let it slide. And really, I think they forgot all about it in the excitement of getting ready to go to Moose Jaw. They were leaving in a week — the day after the

Young Einsteins tryout. I went around the house studying, trying to cram as many facts into my head as I could, and my mom and dad seemed to think of it as just another one of my quirks — like weighing golf balls in spider webs.

But it was no quirk to me. It was serious business. I read dictionaries. I read encyclopedias. I read the Guinness Book of Records. I made notes on index cards and carried them with me everywhere. One day I was stirring spaghetti sauce while reviewing my Famous Explorers card. "The first person to reach the South Pole was Captain Roald Amundsen of Norway," I told my mom.

"Star, watch what you're doing."

"In 1911," I added.

"Star!"

I looked up. There was spaghetti sauce all over the stove. "Whoops."

"Get out. Go. Go outside. Before I strangle you."

I went outside. Mrs. Wentworth was in her garden, watering her flowers. "Hi, Mrs. Wentworth," I called.

"Oh, hello, Starshine," Mrs. Wentworth said. She sounded all stuffed up.

"What's the matter, Mrs. Wentworth? Got a cold?"

"Yes, and another earache," she said, stopping to blow her nose. "Seems like I just can't get rid of them lately."

I remembered that she'd been in bed with an earache just a few weeks ago. My mom had made her some lentil-spinach soup. I'd carried it over to her house and only spilled a little bit. "That's too bad."

Hughie ran over and dropped his ball at my feet. I knelt

down and scratched his ears. "Sorry, boy, I don't have time to throw your ball today. I'm very busy studying."

"Big test coming up?" Mrs. Wentworth said.

"No, I'm trying out for *Young Einsteins*."

I hoped Mrs. Wentworth would say, Oh yes, that delightful show for smart children, but instead she looked blank and said, "What's that?"

I explained.

Mrs. Wentworth said, "That's nice." Then she frowned and aimed the hose at her rose bush. "You get off my roses, you darn aphids."

"Aphids, aphids," I said. I shuffled through my cards until I found the one called Insects. "Did you know, Mrs. Wentworth, that a single cabbage aphid can have 906 million tons of babies in a year?"

Mrs. Wentworth put her hand to her cheek. "Oh, my. I'd better go and buy some bug spray right away."

"I don't think you need to, Mrs. Wentworth," I said. "It was cabbage aphids, not rose aphids." I felt a little peeved. I'd wanted her to be impressed by how smart I was, not worried about bugs.

Hughie picked up his ball and dropped it again. It splotched noisily. "Dogs," I said. "I can tell you about dogs, too, Mrs. Wentworth. The largest litter of puppies ever born was to an American foxhound named Lena. She had twenty-three."

"Twenty-three puppies!" Mrs. Wentworth gasped. "Imagine them popping out, one after another. Pop-pop-pop-pop —"

"They all lived, too."

"What about the mother? Did she live, poor thing?"

"It didn't say," I said.

"And what about milk?" Mrs. Wentworth went on worriedly. "How could she feed all those puppies, I ask you?"

"I don't know, Mrs. Wentworth," I said, gathering up my cards.

"Exhausted, that's what she'd be, the poor dear. *Achoo*!"

"God bless you. I hope you feel better soon, Mrs. Wentworth."

Hughie looked at me reproachfully. "Sorry, Hughie, I'll come back and play when the audition is over, I promise."

"Good luck, dear," Mrs. Wentworth said.

"Thanks, Mrs. Wentworth. I'll need it."

Week Four, I was feeding Goldy-legs katydids. Fred said he wasn't so sure they were a good idea, since katydids live where it's dry and *Nephilas* come from hot, humid places, and maybe *Nephilas* wouldn't have a taste for katydids. But we were running out of flying insects, so I decided to give katydids a try anyway. Goldy-legs seemed to like them — at least she gobbled them all up — but by the end of the week I began to think Fred might have been right. The web didn't look so great.

After a month of doing the experiment, I could pretty much tell from the appearance of the webs how strong they would be. Some had a delicate, feathery look, with lots of space between the strands. Others were tightly woven with thick, ropy threads of silk.

Week Four's web sagged like an out-of-shape volleyball net. And the color wasn't as bright as usual, either, kind of a lemony yellow rather than golden-yellow. Whatever it was that Goldy-legs put in the silk to give it that bright golden hue, she seemed to be a little low on this week.

Sure enough, when it came to the weigh-in, the web was a loser. It only held five golf balls before the sixth one made it rip.

"Phooey!" I said out loud. After a GOLF BALL THRESHOLD of eleven last week, with the moths, I'd had such high hopes. I thought we'd just get better and better. But now we were back to a threshold of five — better than Week One but not as good as Week Two. We were getting worse instead of better.

I knelt down and said, "Goldy-legs, this is no way to help the world get rid of plastic grocery bags."

She waved one leg feebly.

"I know it's not your fault," I said. "I've got to figure out what to feed you. But what? I wish you could tell me."

Goldy-legs just sat there. I didn't know what to try next. And I began to wonder if there really was a magic bug out there somewhere, one bug that could make her web super-strong. And even if there was, would I find it? Would I be the one to help the world get rid of plastic grocery bags? At this rate, it sure didn't look like it.

Chapter Eight

I sat at a table with three other kids — Miranda, Dev and a boy named Mitchell Sorotnik. Mitchell wore a VANCOUVER SOCCER CLUB track suit and had kind of shaggy black hair and he looked like he'd be more at home on a soccer field than on *Young Einsteins*. I hoped he wasn't too smart.

A man and a woman, Jack and June, sat at a table facing us. Jack had short, punky brown hair and a long, pointy nose that reminded me of the Wicked Witch of the West in *The Wizard of Oz*, even though he had a nice, friendly face and there wasn't anything witchy about it. June had curly red hair and lots of freckles all over her face. Both were wearing *Young Einsteins* sweatshirts decorated with pictures of Albert Einstein, his hair frizzing out every which way. I hoped I'd get an Einstein sweatshirt when I got on the show. He was a cool-looking guy.

There was a huge TV screen behind Jack and June and an electric scoreboard with our names. STARSHINE, said my name in lights. I couldn't stop staring at it. Two big cameras were pointed at us. Technicians were fiddling with the lights and mumbling into headsets. Finally a green light went on over the TV screen.

"OK, kids, " June said, "here's what's going to happen. These are the questions." She held up a stack of cards. "Jack and I will take turns reading them out. If you know the answer, push your button." We each had a doorbell-like button in front of us. I pushed mine, just to make sure it worked. BUZZ! It worked.

Jack gave me a look.

June went on, "Whoever hits his or her buzzer first gets to answer the question. If you answer it correctly, you get a point. If someone misses a question and you know the answer, push your button as soon as we've said that's the wrong answer. Then you'll get a chance to answer it."

My eyes strayed to the screen. There I was, flanked by the other kids. I moved in my seat. The me on the screen moved, too. I gave myself a smile. Cheese. I turned sideways to see my dimple. Oops, wrong side. Things were opposite. I turned the other way. There it was. Hello, television-land, it's me, Starshine —

"Starshine? Starshine?" Jack was calling. "Ready?"

"Ready."

"OK, then," June said, picking up the top card. "First question. What is the capital of Prince Edward Island?"

I knew that ! BUZZ! But I was too late. Miranda hit her button first. "Charlottetown," she said.

"Correct," Jack said.

A bell rang for a correct answer and "1" lit up under

Miranda's name on the scoreboard. She flashed a smile.

"Very good," June said."Next question. How many horns did a Triceratops have on its head?"

Triceratops … triceratops … Uncle Beasley, the dinosaur in *The Enormous Egg*, was a triceratops. I tried to remember him from the pictures in the book. There was one horn on his nose …

BUZZ!

"Yes, Mitchell?"

"Three."

"Correct."

Ding! Mitchell got a point.

"Easy," he said."Tri — three. Cera — horn. Ops — eye." He was smart, all right.

"In Guatemala, the currency is also a bird. What is it called?" June asked.

BUZZ! BUZZ! Dev and Miranda both hit their buttons.

"I think Dev was a shade sooner," Jack said. "Dev?"

"Quetzal."

Quetzal? Quetzal?

Now I was the only one without a point. Concentrate, I told myself.

June flipped up a card."What is the part of a bird where it digests its food?"

BUZZ! My finger stabbed the button.

"Yes, Starshine?"

"The grizzle," I said proudly.

Jack and June exchanged a look. Beside me, Mitchell snorted. "I'm sorry, that's wrong," Jack said.

BUZZ!

"Mitchell?"

"The gizzard," he said, clearly pronouncing the "d."

"Correct."

Ding! He got *my* point. Not smart? What was I thinking?

Jack flipped up a card. "There is only one city in the world that straddles two continents. Name the city and the continents."

BUZZ! BUZZ! BUZZ! Miranda, Dev, Mitchell.

Miranda was first. "Istanbul, Turkey. It's in both Europe and Asia."

"Very good, Miranda," Jack said.

What did she do for fun, study atlases?

"What plant is supposed to keep you safe from vampires?"

A plant? How about a gun?

Dev got that one — garlic.

"What is the sum of four times six, plus the difference between twenty and seven, plus the quotient of fifty-four divided by nine?"

Before I could even remember the first part of the question, Mitchell had pressed his button. BUZZ! "Forty-three."

"Correct." Did he have a calculator hidden somewhere?

Ding! I looked at the scoreboard. Dev — three, Mitchell — five, Miranda — eight. Starshine — zero.

OK, it was time to buckle down. Get serious. Get smart. Get a point!

"What red-haired heroine broke her slate chalkboard

over her classmate's head?"

My finger hit the button even before Jack finished reading the question.

"Yes, Starshine?"

"Pippi Longstocking."

Jack and June exchanged a look — again. The other three kids snickered. "Sorry, wrong."

BUZZ!

"Yes, Miranda?"

"Anne of Green Gables."

Pippi Longstocking! How could I? What a dope! I could feel my TV career slipping farther away with every question I missed — with every answer *they* got right. I had to get one. At least one. Just one. Please, God, one.

"What's the name for the fat that keeps a whale warm?"

My finger shot out. BUZZ! "Blooper!" As soon as it was out of my mouth, I knew it was wrong. I knew it was the stupidest thing I'd ever said. It was, in fact, a great big whopping blooper. I wanted to crawl under the table.

"Dev?"

"Blubber."

"Yes, indeed, blubber."

Ding. Another point for Dev. Ding. Another point for Miranda. Ding. Another point for Mitchell.

No points for me.

Zilch.

Nothing.

A big fat zero stared at me from the scoreboard, while their scores went up and up and up. After a while, I didn't even want to answer any more questions, I just wanted to get out of there. Why had I come? Why had I bothered? Why had I thought I was smart enough? Because I was a jerk, that's why. Because I was stupid, dumb, idiotic, dopey, simple-minded … See how clever I am? I thought. Look how many words I can think of that mean the opposite of smart.

Finally, June said, "OK, here's the last question. Of all the spiders in the world, which one spins the largest web and what color is the web?"

BUZZZZZ!! "I know that! I know that!"

Jack and June exchanged a look as if to say, Yeah, sure. "Yes, Starshine?"

"The spider is the *Nephila*. And the web is golden yellow."

"Correct!" They sounded amazed.

My zero changed into a one. Miranda flashed me a smile. I knew she was trying to be nice, but I couldn't manage a smile back. Not with the the final scores staring me in the face: Miranda — twenty-three, Mitchell — twenty-five, Dev — twenty. Starshine — one.

June started talking about how well we'd done and how pleased they were to have so many good contestants to choose from. I didn't wait to hear the speech. I ran outside to where my dad was waiting in the parking lot and jumped into the car. "I want to go home. Now!" I yelled, slamming the door shut.

When we got home, my mom took one look at my face and held out her arms. "Not so good, huh?" she said. I shook my head against her chest. My dad hugged me from behind, making a Starshine sandwich. It felt good but it didn't take away the awful feeling inside.

"How bad was it?" my mom said, pulling away and looking at me.

"The only question I got was one about spiders."

"Oh, brother," my dad said.

I nodded, my eyes filling with tears. "I'm so stupid —"

"You are not!" my mom said.

"Just because you missed a few questions —" my dad began.

"I didn't miss a few! I missed them all! I blew it. Completely. I looked like an idiot. I *was* an idiot." I started bawling, my face in my hands.

"Star, honey, don't cry," my mom said, patting me.

"It's OK, honey, it's OK," my dad said, ruffling my hair.

I sobbed. "Th-they w-were s-so s-s-smart."

My mom stroked me. I sobbed. My dad said, "There's smart and then there's smart, Star."

"Wh-wh-what do you mean?" I blubbered.

"Just because you're not a walking encyclopedia, doesn't mean you're not smart," he said.

Like Mitchell, I thought.

"Some people can do math problems in their head. Some people can't. But they can recite poetry," my mom added.

"Some people can fix car engines just by listening to them," my dad said.

"Some people are good spellers."

I'm a good speller — I don't even have to try.

"Some people know all about spiders."

It was true — I knew I was smart in other ways — but I also knew they were just trying to make me feel better. I hate it when people try to make me feel better. It makes me feel worse. But I stopped crying. I was cried out anyway.

My mom wiped my eyes with her shirt. "So, what were the questions like? Were they really hard?"

I nodded. "Killers."

"Like what?"

"Like, what is both a bird and a coin in Guatemala?"

"That's easy, the quetzal," my dad said.

I glared at him.

"But we visited Guatemala, Starshine," he said apologetically. "That's the only reason I know that."

"What else, honey?" my mom asked.

"Um … what's the part of a chicken where it digests its food?"

"The gizzard, of course," she said, then clapped her hand over her mouth. "Sorry!"

"Guess what I said."

"What?"

"The grizzle." In spite of myself, I started giggling.

"The grizzle?" my mom said, laughing.

"You didn't," my dad chuckled.

"And you know what I said for a whale's fat?" I added, figuring I might as well let it all out.

"What?"

"Blooper."

"Blooper?" my mom shrieked.

"Blooper?" my dad roared with laughter. "Oh, Star, you're too much."

I laughed, too. It felt good. But it was the kind of laughing that's very close to crying.

Just then the phone rang. My mom answered it. "Hello? Oh, hi, Phyl. Yeah, 10:30. We'll be there."

That was my mom's sister, Aunt Phyllis. My grandma was coming to look after Peggy and me while my mom and dad were in Saskatchewan getting their prize. Aunt Phyl was taking Grandma to the airport, so I guessed she was calling to tell my mom everything had gone OK and Grandma was on her way. She was coming late tonight, and my mom and dad were leaving for Moose Jaw in the morning.

My mom grinned. "Yes, we're so excited … They've got quite a gala ceremony planned … I can't wait … Just think, Phyl, Peter and me in the spotlight! It's such a thrill! … Thanks … OK, 'bye."

My mom hung up, then looked at her watch. "Gosh, Pete, we'd better get moving. We've got a million things to do before my mother gets here."

They started talking about their trip, what to pack, what kind of shoes, what to wear to the gala dinner …

I slipped upstairs to my room. There were all my study cards, neatly stacked on the bed. SCIENCE FACTS … ANIMAL FACTS … MATH FACTS … I swept them onto the floor and flopped onto my bed, my chin in my hands.

I'd blown it — again. Blown my last chance to shine, my last chance to outdo Peggy, my last chance to get on television. Peggy had a TV contract, a Kitten Krunchies Girl Fan Club, a new wardrobe and the instant attention of everybody she met. And me? I had one point on *Young Einsteins*. And an allergy. Oh, yeah. Couldn't forget that. I had that, all right.

Chapter Nine

Things didn't go well with Grandma.

She had been there about five minutes when she let out a shriek. I came hurtling down the stairs from my room. "What's the matter, Grandma?"

The refrigerator door was wide open and she was pointing at something inside. "Wh-what are those disgusting creatures?"

Uh-oh. I knew there was something I was supposed to warn her about. "Wasps, Grandma."

"Wasps! What are they doing in the refrigerator?"

I explained about the experiment. She put her hand on my shoulder, shaking her head. "Oh, Starshine, what am I going to do with you? You're such a sweet girl. Couldn't you get interested in sewing? Or stamps? Now tell me, what's wrong with stamps?"

"Nothing, Grandma. I just like spiders."

We have this conversation every time my grandma comes. She seems to think that liking spiders isn't quite normal. She's always trying to get me interested in other things. One time when I was little she brought a suitcase full of dolls. I hated dolls. Another time it was macramé. I got the yarn into hopeless knots. Then she brought a kit called *How to Make Papier-Mâché Puppets in Five Easy Steps*, and we made a set of damp puppet people that looked like mouldy potatoes. Even Grandma didn't want to play with them.

None of her plans worked. I stayed interested in spiders. But she's never given up hope that I'll find a normal hobby someday.

"Must the wasps be in the refrigerator, Starshine?" she said.

"Yes, they must," I said. "They have to be fresh or Goldy-legs — or the spider won't eat them." She gave a slight shudder. "But I'll push them back here behind the horseradish, so you don't have to look at them. We never eat horseradish anyway."

She sighed, looking sorrowfully at me.

Just then Peggy came in, holding a long cardboard tube. It was from Talent Trail Studios. "Look at what I got, Grandma!" Inside there was a huge poster of Peggy in her Kitten Krunchies outfit, holding Poopsie. The poster was signed, "To the kitten of my heart — Arthur P. Molesworth, President, Kitten Krunchies Inc."

"Peggy, how precious!" Grandma said. "It's a wonderful picture of you — your cheeks are so rosy, and you look so pretty in that dress. I must hang it up right away." And she did, right on the kitchen wall, so Peggy's smiling face could beam down on us as we ate our granola.

"Just think, my own grand-daughter, a TV star!" Grandma said, ruffling Peggy's curls adoringly. "Not that I'm surprised, mind you. Ever since you were tiny, Pumpkin, you had that certain something. That star quality, I guess. Didn't she, Starshine? Wasn't Peggy just made for television?"

"Yes, Grandma," I muttered, and ran from the room.

The next day, there was another burglary in our neighbourhood. This one was only two blocks away. It was the silver thief again, and he robbed a man named Mr. Paluzzo. He stole Mr. Paluzzo's collection of silver coins from the Yukon. The newspaper said Mr. Paluzzo's coins were a hundred years old and worth over a thousand dollars. "My grandpapa rode a horse all the way to the Yukon to work in the mines," Mr. Paluzzo said in the newspaper. "And for what? So some crook could steal his silver coins!"

When my grandmother heard about the burglary, she threw her arms around my sister. "He'll kidnap Peggy next!"

"What a great idea, Grandma!" I said. "How can we get hold of him?"

Grandma frowned. I could tell she didn't think that was funny. Neither did I. I meant it. "Don't worry, Grandma, he's stealing silver, not kids," I said.

"Peggy is worth more than silver!" Grandma said, holding Peggy tight.

No kidding. She acted as though Peggy were made of solid gold. The little brat could do no wrong. With me, it was, "Starshine, pick up your sweatshirt off the floor." With Peggy, it was, "Come here, Pumpkin, and Grandma'll tell you a story." When I showed Grandma my Social Studies report on the Beaver — (It was called "The Beaver: Toothy Symbol of Canada" and I'd got an A- on it. I would've got an A but I had a little trouble drawing the beaver's teeth. They looked like snow shovels.) — she said, "Mmm-hmm, very nice," but when Peggy brought home some woven paper thing she'd done at preschool, Grandma said it was a masterpiece and hung it over the fireplace mantel.

I wished I could find that burglar and give him our address.

At school on Monday, Miranda and Dev announced they'd both been chosen to be on *Young Einsteins*. Miranda must have said something to Ms. Fung ahead of time, because she didn't ask me how *I'd* done, thank goodness, but only shot me a sympathetic look. I stared down at my desk.

"Why don't you ask Einstein Shapiro what her score was," Jimmy snickered.

I felt my cheeks burn.

"You shut up, Jimmy Tyler!" Julie hissed.

Jimmy held up his finger. "Two plus two equals five — duh!"

"I'll get you on the playground," Julie swore.

"That'll be quite enough from you, James, or I'll see you after school," Ms. Fung said, and Jimmy shut up. But it didn't matter. Everyone knew.

Ms. Fung turned back to Miranda and Dev. "Who are the other contestants?"

"Mitchell Sorotnik," Dev said. Of course.

"And a girl named Tabitha Tan," Miranda said. "She's only nine but they're letting her in because she had the highest score of anybody who tried out."

"My, my," Ms. Fung said, "she must be very bright."

No kidding. A regular Einstein. I was glad I hadn't had to compete against her. She probably would have got my one spider question.

"When can we expect to see you on television?" Ms. Fung asked.

"We're shooting a pilot this weekend," Miranda said. "We'll start appearing on the show the week after that."

"Well, let's have a big round of applause for our two very own Young Einsteins," Ms. Fung said.

Everybody clapped. Oh great, I thought. Now I can watch *another* TV show I'm not on.

Two nights later, *The Wizard of Oz* was on television. Julie invited me to watch it at her house. I didn't want to. It wasn't that I minded that she was on and I wasn't — I'd finally admitted that I really couldn't dance or sing — but I didn't feel like being reminded that I'd blown the chance to outshine Peggy. But I didn't want to hurt Julie's feelings, so I went.

What a scene! Both sets of Julie's grandparents were there, along with about twenty aunts, uncles and cousins — and that was on top of Julie and her three brothers and her mom and dad. Mrs. Wong had made enough food to feed the entire neighbourhood. There were chocolate chip cookies, tiny eggrolls, bacon-lettuce-and-tomato sandwiches, preserved duck eggs, fried chicken, pork balls and Rice Krispie squares. Kind of a Canadian-Chinese smorgasbord. Everybody helped themselves and there was the clink of plates and the chatter of English and Chinese and laughter and the cousins chasing each other around and their moms scolding them to sit down and Mrs. Wong telling everybody she would be insulted if they didn't eat more.

At eight o'clock sharp everybody squeezed into the living room as the show came on. In the opening credits, the names of the Munchkins rolled by. THOMAS THORNBERRY, JENNIFER WINSTON, JULIE WONG.

"There she is!"

"That's our Julie!"

"Did you see that!"

Julie grinned.

It took a while for the Munchkins to appear, but finally Dorothy's house landed in Munchkinland, and there they were, crowding around Dorothy and Toto, jumping and cheering and shouting, "The Wicked Witch is dead! The Wicked Witch is dead!"

"See me? See me?" Julie said.

"Where?"

"There you are!"

"How cute she looks!"

She did look cute, in her checkered dress with the puffy sleeves and her floppy hat and her green boots. She looked happy and Munchkin-like. She had presence.

"How graceful!" Julie's grandma said.

"Listen to that beautiful voice," said one of the Uncle Wei's.

"But Uncle, we're all singing together," Julie pointed out, winking at me.

Uncle Wei shook his head emphatically. "I hear *you*, Julie, I hear *you*."

Julie and I giggled.

When the movie was over, the living room exploded with enthusiastic comments.

"How wonderful!"

"Julie, you're a star!"

"Those are the best Munchkins I've ever seen!"

"Three cheers for Julie!"

Julie turned from relative to relative, beaming. I was happy for her. She deserved all the good things they were saying. But after a while, I couldn't help thinking how different things would be if I had made it, too. That would have taken Peggy down a notch or two.

When I left, I gave Julie a hug. "You were terrific, Jule."

"Really?"

"Cross my heart."

And I meant it. But I also wished I'd been on there, too,

and I'd been terrific, too, so I could show Peggy, show my mom and dad, show Grandma, show Mr. Brintmorgan, show everyone. And now I'd used up all my chances. Tears stung my eyes. I didn't want Julie to think it was her. I turned quickly and ran home.

After all that, I was looking forward to the Week Five web weigh-in, hoping something good would happen. Julie was over, and when we went out back there was a pile of wasp heads on the floor. Usually Goldy-legs chomped down every bit of a bug. The leftover heads weren't a good sign. Neither was the web. It was droopy and pale yellow, even worse-looking than the katydid one. Goldy-legs just sat there when I removed the web, as if to say, Go ahead, take it, it's a lousy web anyway.

"I have a sinking feeling," I said.

"You have a sinking web," Julie added.

She got the RECORD OF WEB STRENGTH ready and put the first golf ball in. It held, barely.

"Number two," she said, gently placing the second golf ball next to the first. It sagged, but held.

"Three." The web didn't rip, it just kind of collapsed with a sigh, and the golf balls rolled to the floor.

"Oh, no!" I said.

"Gosh," Julie said. Even she sounded alarmed.

I looked over her shoulder as she filled out the GOLF BALL THRESHOLD. "Four, seven, eleven, six, two," I read aloud.

"It went up but then it went down," Julie pointed out.

"I can see that," I snapped.

"Sor — ry."

"Oh, I didn't mean it, Jule," I said miserably. "I just don't know what's wrong. This is a disaster. A catastrophe. My experiment is dying." A thought came to me and I gasped.

"What?" Julie said.

"Maybe Goldy-legs is sick. Maybe *she's* dying!"

"Oh, no!"

I knelt down and whispered to Goldy-legs, "Listen, girl, you can't die. Not before I find the bug that can save the environment! Please! Maybe it was just indigestion. Maybe wasps don't agree with you. I don't blame you. I couldn't stomach wasps, either. But please, Goldy-legs, hold on. I'll find you something really yummy this time. Something you'll love. I don't know what, but I'll find it. Trust me. Just hang in there. OK?"

She started spinning a new web. A feather-light thread of golden silk trailed out behind her. She turned toward me as if to say, One more chance.

Chapter Ten

"Mom! Dad!"

Until I saw them coming through the sliding doors at the airport, I didn't realize how much I'd missed them. My dad was wearing his old jeans and UBC sweatshirt, and my mom had on her long swirly paisley skirt and they were all wrinkled and untidy and looked just like themselves. They held out their arms and I rushed in. I'd had a rotten week, but now everything would be OK.

"Star! Peggy! Mom!" My mom tried to hug all of us at once and we were a crush of cheeks and kisses.

"Mommy! Daddy!" Peggy said, jumping up and down. "I was a good girl!"

Everybody laughed. "Now, why does that make me suspicious?" my mom said.

"She was as good as gold," Grandma said with a smile. "But, boy, am I exhausted. I've forgotten what it's like. How do you find the energy, Joanie?"

"By going away and leaving it all to you," my mom said, and everybody laughed again.

On the way to the car, Peggy insisted on riding in the luggage cart, which my dad was pushing, and my mom had her arm linked with Grandma's, so I was left alone. I tagged behind, listening to Mom tell Grandma — who was staying a few more days so she could visit with all of us — that she and my dad had made the front page of the *Moose Jaw Herald* and had bought up all the spare copies in town.

We piled into the car. "So what was the ceremony like?" Grandma asked, but before Mom or Dad could answer, Peggy interrupted. "Mommy, Daddy, guess what! I got a big, big picture. Of me and Poopsie."

"You did?" my mom said.

"The cat food company sent an adorable poster," Grandma explained. "Wait till you see it. You could die, she's so cute."

"I can't wait," my mom said, smiling at Peggy.

"And I got more letters. Bunches of them," Peggy added.

"One little boy asked if she would marry him," Grandma said, smiling.

Mom and Dad burst out laughing. "Well, I don't blame him, Pumpkin," my dad said. "I'd ask you myself if I weren't already married."

"Mommy wouldn't like that," Peggy said in a cutesy voice.

Grandma pinched her cheek. "Is she smart or what?"

Or what, I thought.

Mom turned and looked at me. "You're quiet, Star. How was your week?"

"OK ,"I said. If you didn't count Miranda and Dev making *Young Einsteins* and watching Julie on *The Wizard of Oz* and only two golf balls and Grandma favouring Peggy all the time. Otherwise it was great.

We pulled into the driveway. My mom sighed. "Oh, it's good to be home."

When we got inside, Dad said, "Everybody go into the living room and we'll show you the solar cooker. It's quite a marvel."

"First," Grandma interrupted, "you've got to see this." She led my mom and dad into the kitchen and stood them in front of the Kitten Krunchies poster.

"Peggy, how precious!" my mom said. "And from the Chairman, no less. My, my, young lady, you *are* an important person."

My dad scooped her into his arms. "Is that beautiful girl really my daughter?"

"Yup," Peggy said, grinning.

He carried her into the living room, then stopped in front of the fireplace. "And look at this weaving! Who could have done such beautiful weaving, I wonder?"

"Me!" Peggy shouted.

My dad laughed and kissed her. I wished I was four again and could be held like that.

My mom unwrapped the solar cooker. It was about as big as our toaster oven, all shiny inside except for the clear parts. "Does it really work?" I said.

"Sure," my dad said. He looked outside. "I think it's sunny enough, don't you, Joanie?"

My mom looked up. "Can't hurt to try." They put the solar cooker out front and got a little pot of water and put it inside, and sure enough, after about ten minutes the water boiled and my mom made tea in the new golden yellow teapot she'd made recently. She was on a golden yellow glaze kick, inspired by Goldy-legs. Everything was that colour — plates, cups, bowls, vases. I called it her *Nephila* Phase.

When everyone was settled with their tea, Grandma said, "So, tell us about the gala."

"Oh, Mom, it was great!" my mom said.

"Everybody went crazy over the sculpture," my dad added.

"They just loved it —"

"All the Moose Jaw bigwigs were there —"

"We must have shaken two hundred hands, I'm not exaggerating —"

"And the newspaper reporters were flashing cameras in our faces —"

"Oh, I forgot!" my mom said, jumping up. "Be right back." She ran out of the room and I heard her rummaging around in her suitcase and then she came back with an armful of copies of the *Moose Jaw Herald*. "Look!"

There they were on the front page, my dad in a sportcoat with a tie that was about five inches wide with flowers on it, all bunched up at the neck, as if he'd forgotten how to tie a tie, and my mom in a long batik dress and Birkenstocks. They were both grinning, holding a plaque or something in their hands.

"Oh, Joanie, I'm so proud," my grandma said, dabbing at her eyes with a handkerchief.

Peggy hugged my dad. "You're famous, too — just like me."

My dad laughed. "Yes, Pumpkin, just like you."

"So, my little Pumpkin, tell us about your fan mail," my mom said, pulling Peggy onto her lap.

"Well, one said I was bee-you-ti-ful, and one said how old are you and when is your birthday, and one ..."

On and on she went, my parents hanging on every word, Grandma adding bits that Peggy forgot, Peggy smiling her precious smile and looking around to make sure no one was missing a thing — as if they would. I felt invisible. I felt jealous and mean. A lump came into my throat. Finally, holding back the tears, I ran out of the living room, up the stairs, and flopped onto my bed. Then I sobbed.

A minute later there was a knock on the door. My parents came in. "Starshine, honey, what's the matter?" my mom said.

"Nothing," I wept.

"Come on, Star," my dad said, "what's wrong?"

"Everything!" I blubbered into my pillow.

They sat down on either side of me. I tried to hold it in, but it all came blundering out. "I-I-I was su-su-supposed to be on T-T-TV, but P-Peggy took it away from me ..." I gulped. "A-and then J-Julie got on the W-Wizard uh-of Oz and I d-didn't," I went on, my face still in the pillow, "and th-then I b-bombed on the *Y-Young Einsteins* ..." I burst into fresh sobs. "A-and G-G-Grandma only p-p-paid attention to P-Peggy, and G-Goldy-legs's web only held two g-g-golf b-b-balls, and I ne-never got on T-T-V!"

"Oh, sweetheart," my mom said, stroking my hair.

"Starry-Starry-Star," my dad said, calling me by my baby nickname.

"You poor thing," my mom said.

"Starry-Starry-Star ..."

I cried, feeling all my unhappiness in the pit of my stomach. Slowly I stopped sobbing and just sniffled.

"Star, honey, what's the big deal about getting on television?" my dad asked.

"Peggy," I said into my pillow.

"Peggy?" my mom said. "What do you mean?"

Not looking at them, I said, "She's always the centre of attention. Always. I wanted to be, for once. And Mr. Brintmorgan noticed me and I thought, Finally! But she stole it anyway." I started crying again. "And th-then I w-wanted to try again to g-get on T-T-V, to sh-show you that I was ju-ju-just as good, but it d-didn't work, n-nothing worked, it ne-ne-never does —"

"Starshine," my mom said in a voice that sounded like *she* was going to cry, "what do you mean, show us you were just as good?"

I took a big sniff. "No one ever notices me. It's always Peggy, Peggy, Peggy. She's so — CUTE!"

"Of course she's cute," my dad said. "She's four years old."

"And she knows exactly how to get everybody's attention," my mom added.

"Yeah!" I yelled. "It's not fair."

My dad ruffed my hair. "It comes with the turf, Star. You were that cute when you were four."

"I was?" I looked at him, wiping my eyes on my sleeve.

"Sure. In a few years she'll be a funny-looking seven-year-old with no teeth, and you'll be a raving beauty of a teenager."

"Yeah, right. That'll be the day."

"Trust me," my dad said. "You will. Too soon."

I didn't believe him. Me, a raving beauty? Steal the spotlight from Peggy? Impossible. "But she's always showing off," I argued. "She's so good at it."

"And you're not?" my mom said, bending down so I had to look her in the eye.

"No," I admitted. "I wish I was."

"But then you wouldn't be Starshine," my dad said.

I looked at him. "What do you mean?"

"I mean you're not a show-off. You're not a phony. That's the beauty of you, Star. You're real. You care about things. You hold them in your heart."

Tears filled my eyes, hearing that. I'd never thought of myself that way. No one had ever said it before. But it was true. My dad had known something true about the inside of me.

"And everyone who knows you, knows that," my mom added.

That set me off again. "No, they don't! Look at Grandma.

It's Peggy this, and Peggy that, all day long. She doesn't even know I exist."

"Oh yeah?" my dad said. "Then how come she hasn't stopped raving about everything you did this week?"

"L-like what?"

"Like the A- on your Beavers report," my mom said with a smile.

"And how you helped around the house."

"And your winning goal in soccer."

"And how adorable you look in the new pajamas she brought you."

"And how you moved the wasps behind the horseradish," my mom said, laughing. "She said, 'That nut! I could eat her up!'"

"She did?"

"Just because she was all wrapped up in looking after a demanding four-year-old doesn't mean she didn't notice every wonderful thing about you."

A big chunk of rottenness left my stomach. So Grandma *had* noticed me. I hadn't known. I felt funny inside.

"You know, Star, you remind me of myself," my mom said with a smile.

"What do you mean?"

"I felt exactly the same way about Aunt Phyl when I was your age."

"You did?"

She nodded. "I was so jealous. There I was, the older sister, always a good girl. Quiet, studious, doing what I was supposed to. And there was my little sister, with her dimples and her giggle and her temper tantrums and her naughty, adorable ways. I felt like wallpaper next to her."

"But — but you're so pretty!" I said. "And smart. And talented."

"Ah, but I didn't know it then," my mom said with a laugh. "I only saw how cute my little sister was. How she had everybody wrapped around her little finger. I couldn't stand her!"

"But you're best friends now," I said.

"Of course."

My mom just let that hang in the air for a minute. I thought about it — and then a wild thought came to me. "No way!" I shouted.

My mom and dad both laughed. "You and Peggy won't be good friends for a long time yet," my dad said. "Not till you find out she's jealous of you, too."

"That's impossible!" Still, I was feeling a lot better. Imagine my mom feeling just like I did!

My dad held out his arms and I snuggled in. "Star, Peggy could win the Academy Award, and she still wouldn't be one bit more special than you are."

"Or more loved," my mom added.

"And you certainly don't have to be on television to be special to us."

"Of course not," my mom agreed.

"You're smart."

"You're pretty."

"You're funny."

"You have — er — unusual interests."

I smiled.

"And we love you whether you're on TV or not," my dad said and they both hugged me.

"Well, that's good, because I've blown every chance I had, and probably every chance I'll ever have again," I said with a laugh.

"You never know," my mom said. "Maybe something incredible will happen to you tomorrow and you'll get on TV after all."

"Yeah, right," I said, but I was smiling.

"Maybe not," she went on. "Maybe you'll never get on TV in your whole life. Maybe you'll just be an ordinary person. But you'll still be you, and that's special enough for us."

They hugged and kissed me, and I hugged and kissed them back, and they left. I lay back on my soggy pillow. I felt a lot better. I was still a bit jealous of Peggy — I had to admit it — but I didn't feel so rotten.

It still would be neat to be on television, though. Maybe someday. Maybe not, as my mom said. But maybe so.

Chapter Eleven

On the way home from school, I stopped off at the bait shop.

"Hi, Starshine," said Fred. "How'd it go with the wasps?"

"Worse than the katydids."

"No! Really?"

I nodded. "Two golf balls."

"Two! Gosh, that's terrible." He shook his head. "I wonder why. *Nephilas* should be used to wasps. Say —" He stopped and shook his head. "No."

"What?"

"Nothing."

"WHAT?"

"Oh, I was just thinking," He gave a forced smile. "— that maybe it was the spider. You know, maybe she's under the weather or something. But —" He tried to chuckle. "— I'm sure that's not it."

"That's exactly what I thought," I said gloomily. "Oh, Fred, what'll I do? There's only one week left. Even if Goldy-legs isn't dying, what should I give her? What can I feed her that'll shoot the golf ball total back up again?"

Fred leaned on the counter, his chin on his hands. "I don't know. And I've got some bad news for you, Starshine. You've already tried all the flying insects I've got."

"I have?"

He nodded glumly. "Just crawlers left now."

"But — but flying bugs are what orb-weavers eat!" I said. "I don't know if Goldy-legs would even look at a crawling insect."

"I know."

"Oh, no! What am I going to do?"

"I don't know, Starshine," Fred said. He looked as upset as I felt. "Why don't you have a look around and see if anything inspires you?"

I wandered the aisles, looking into the cages. He was right. The only insects we hadn't tried yet were crawling ones. Slugs slimed across their jars at about one inch an hour. Hornworms rolled into little balls, like curled-up commas. Termites burrowed into sawdust. Cater-pillars inched along branches, their hair ruffling. Ants struggled under their load of a bread crumb. Not one of them would make a decent meal for a spider.

Finally I stopped in front of the maggot jar. They were squirming around in a sickening pile. They were gross. They were squishy. They were slimy. One pop and all their disgusting insides would come oozing out. They certainly weren't on the regular menu for *Nephilas,* but for some reason I thought they might work. Maybe all their sticky insides would make Goldy-legs's silk stickier. So the threads would hold together better.

"Fred," I said. "I'm going to try maggots."

"Any particular reason?"

"I'm desperate," I said with a grin.

"Well, maybe they'll do the trick," he said, shaking some into a bottle.

"I hope so."

"Me, too. Good luck, Starshine. Let me know what happens, OK?"

"OK. 'Bye, Fred."

It was late by the time I got home. I expected to get into trouble — I'd forgotten to mention that I was stopping at the bait store. I came in the back door and heard the sound of crying from the living room. Gee, my mom must be really upset! I hurried in. It wasn't my mom, it was Mrs. Wentworth, and she was sniffling into a handkerchief, my mom patting her on the shoulder.

"What's wrong, Mrs. Wentworth?" I said, dropping my pack on the floor.

She fluttered a hand. "I have to go into the hospital tomorrow."

Oh gosh. Maybe it was really life-threatening, and that's why she was crying. "What for?"

"To have my adenoids removed."

"Your adenoids?"

She nodded, dabbing her eyes. "They're inflamed. That's why I keep getting all these earaches."

"Oh."

"And my doctor assures me that having my adenoids out will fix my snoring, too."

"Your snoring?"

"Yes, it's quite bad. Used to keep Mr. Wentworth awake all night. But — but —" Mrs. Wentworth started sniffling again.

"Are you scared of the operation, Mrs. Wentworth, is that it?" I said, taking her hand. "Listen, I had my adenoids out when I was little. It's not so bad. You get a sore throat, but it only lasts a few days —"

"No, no," she interrupted. "I'm not worried about myself. It's Hughie." And she broke out into sobs.

Then I remembered. Hughie had just had an operation on his paw. Actually, it was his own fault. He'd been a bad dog. Mrs. Wentworth had made brownies, his favourite, in a glass baking pan. Hughie reached up onto the counter for a bite and accidently knocked the pan down and it broke and he got a piece of glass in his paw and had to have it cut out. So now he was all bandaged up and had to take medicine and everything.

"Mrs. Wentworth is worried about who will take care of Hughie while she's in the hospital," my mom said.

"I couldn't bear to put him in a kennel," Mrs. Wentworth sobbed. "They'd take good care of him, but they wouldn't luh-luh-*love* him."

My mom looked at me. "I was just telling Mrs. Wentworth that you'd be happy to look after Hughie for a few days," she said.

"Sure, I'd love to."

"And I was also telling her that you wouldn't *think* of taking payment for it," my mom added, giving me a look over Mrs. Wentworth's head.

"Uh — of course not," I said weakly.

Mrs. Wentworth dried her eyes. "And I was just saying that I'd want to pay you what I would have had to pay a kennel. It's only fair."

Well, I could certainly see her point. But my mom said quickly, "And I was just telling Mrs. Wentworth that that's what neighbours are for. So I don't want to hear another word." The way she said it, it was final. Not that I cared, really. I didn't mind taking care of Hughie for free. I played with him all the time anyway. Though a little cash wouldn't have hurt. I was saving up for a cool Spiders of the World T-shirt I'd seen advertised in the *Arach-News*. But that was OK. I was glad to do Mrs. Wentworth a favour.

She seemed to see that my mom meant it, too. She sighed and said, "Oh, thank you, Joan. Thank you, Starshine. You don't know what this means to me, knowing that Hughie will be able to stay in his own home. I'm sure he'll get better much faster than if he had to go to a strange place."

My mom patted her on the shoulder. "Don't worry about a thing, Mrs. Wentworth. You just get better yourself."

Mrs. Wentworth smiled and got up to leave. I went home with her so she could give me the key. When we got inside, Hughie got up to greet us and his long black tail wagged, but only half-heartedly, as if it just didn't have any oomph. He limped a few steps, holding the bandaged paw stiffly in front of him, then flopped down in his basket, his brown eyes looking mournfully at me.

"Poor Hughie," I said. I scratched his ears and he sighed contentedly. Then Mrs. Wentworth showed me where Hughie's food was, and his medicine, and the vet's phone number just in case, and gave me instructions. "OK, Mrs. Wentworth," I said. "Good luck with your adenoids. Tell them to give you lots of popsicles. It's the only thing you'll feel like eating anyway. And don't worry, I'll take good care of Hughie."

"Thank you, Starshine," she said, and I left.

When I got home I remembered about the maggots. They were still in my pack. They should go into the fridge. I got the jar and walked across the kitchen. My mom was busy mixing something at the counter. I went over to see what it was, hoping it was cookies or something yummy.

There were two bowls on the counter. One was full of blackstrap molasses. The other bowl had a yellowish-grey powdery mixture. I looked at the open containers on the counter. Brewer's yeast, kelp powder and oat bran. That must be the yellowish grey stuff. I strongly hoped my mom wasn't going to mix the two bowls together, but I had a sinking feeling she was. She's the queen of the health food freaks.

"Whatcha making, Mom?"

She pointed to a recipe in her *Organic Panic Cookbook*. "Super Nutro Bombs."

"Super what?"

"They're super-high-energy nutrition balls," she explained.

"Are they to eat? Or explode?"

"Hah, hah, very funny."

"Why are they called bombs? Do you drop them on your enemies?"

She tried to hide her smile. "No, young lady, they're called bombs because they're so powerful. It says here they deliver a megaton of nutrition."

"Wham! Boom! Crash!" I said, making exploding noises.

"Now, now," my mom said. "I figured they'd be just the thing for Mrs. Wentworth when she gets home from the hospital. With these Super Nutro Bombs, she'll be back on her feet in no time."

"And running to the bathroom to puke," I added, making rude noises.

"Why, you smart aleck," she laughed, giving me a swat on the bottom. She caught me off balance and I stumbled forward. My arm jerked. The top flew off the maggot jar and the maggots tumbled into the molasses.

"Uh-oh."

"Starshine, what was that?"

I was afraid to tell her. "Maggots."

"WHAT!!"

"It wasn't my fault! You bumped me!"

"GET THEM OUT OF THERE!"

I'd already reached for the big mixing spoon. "I'm trying, I'm trying!"

My mom grabbed a spoon, and we both started flailing and poking and slopping blackstrap molasses all over the place. "There's one," I shouted.

"Disgusting!" my mom said.

"I've got another one!"

"Maggots! Oh my God!"

"Get in there, you."

"I got one. No, I lost it," my mom said, dragging her spoon through the molasses.

"There, I've got them! I think I have them all," I said. The maggots, shiny and black, squirmed in the spoon.

"Wait, let me do it! You'll drop them," my mom said, pushing me aside.

She reached for the spoon. Her elbow caught my arm. The spoon shot up in the air and landed in the other bowl. The maggots, miraculously still alive, started tunneling into the brewer's yeast-kelp powder-oat bran mixture.

"Oh my God!" my mom yelled.

"Look what you made me do!"

"What *I* made you do! If your arm hadn't been in the way —"

"I had them! I had them!"

"MAGGOTS! Oh God, I'm going to be sick." She flung open the door and ran to the porch, leaning over the railing, taking deep breaths. I took advantage of her absence to fish the maggots out of the dry mixture. Because of the sticky molasses, they were now caked in powder. They looked like honey-roasted peanuts. Wriggling honey-roasted peanuts. I put them back in the jar.

My mom came in, looking pale but fortunately not throwing up. We took one look at each other and burst out laughing.

"Maggots!" she said.

"Super Nutro Bombs!" I said.

We roared.

"Maggot Bombs!"

"Super Protein Nutro Bombs!"

We laughed and laughed, finally wiping our eyes and looking at the mess. There were splats of blackstrap molasses on the walls, clumps of yellowish grey powder on the floor.

I looked at the jar of maggots and quickly stopped laughing. "Mom, what am I going to do? These are for Goldy-legs. It's the last week. My last chance to make the experiment work!"

My mom glanced at the clock. "I don't know, honey. It's too late to go back to the bait store now. I guess you'll have to feed her one of those for today and get a new batch tomorrow."

"But I can't! I'll poison her."

"Don't get carried away, Starshine. After all, the ingredients are all organic."

"Spiders don't eat blackstrap molasses and brewer's yeast."

"Well, what else are you going to do?"

She had a point. I took the jar of maggots and went out to the porch. I crouched down beside Goldy-legs. "Listen, old girl, I'm really sorry about this — it was an accident — I hope it doesn't taste too bad — this stuff is good for you, you know — well, here goes." I picked a maggot out of the jar and placed it in the corner of the web. Goldy-legs paused for a moment. She waved her front legs around — that's how spiders smell — and then she ran, and I mean *ran*, and ate the maggot in one bite. She didn't even stop to paralyze it or wrap it in silk. She just gobbled it down. Then she started weaving.

I looked at the bomb-encrusted maggots and then I looked at Goldy-legs and then I looked back at the maggots. Then I ran back into the kitchen, shouting, "Mom, don't throw that recipe away, whatever you do!"

Taking care of Hughie was easy. Every day I let myself in by the kitchen door, filled his food and water bowls, and gave him his medicine. Then I let him out so he could go to the bathroom. He always paused at the top of the steps and looked at me pitifully as if to say, Carry me? But I couldn't carry Hughie even if I'd wanted to — he was too heavy. I'd say, "Go on, Hughie," and he'd limp down the six steps as if he were making a great sacrifice, do his business, then give me the same pitiful look at the bottom of the steps. "Come on, Hughie," I'd say, and he'd limp like a martyr up the six steps and flop down in his basket.

He also wasn't eating as much as usual. He seemed kind of dopey, as though he were half-asleep. The saddest thing was, when he got outside, there was his soggy, chewed-up tennis ball lying on the grass, but he didn't even look at it. That worried me. Hughie wasn't Hughie if he wasn't shoving that disgusting ball in my hand, his tail going a mile a minute.

I told my mom, but she said not to worry. She said the vet had probably put something in Hughie's medicine to purposely slow him down, so he'd take it easy while his paw was healing.

I hoped so. I hated seeing Hughie like this. The old Hughie might have been a pain in the neck, panting his horrible dog breath on you and practically knocking you down with his tail and pestering you to play fetch, but that was Hughie.

After Goldy-legs had gobbled down the first maggot, I decided to feed her more of the bomb-coated maggots, just to see what would happen. She ate the second one just as eagerly, as if it was the most delicious treat in the world and she couldn't get enough.

And the web! After a couple of days I noticed that it was different. It was thick and tightly woven, and it stretched firmly across the porch corner without sagging at all. It was a deeper, brighter yellow than the other webs, like the color of my mom's new glaze.

When Julie was over one day, I took her around back and showed her. "Holy cow! What are you feeding her?"

"You're not going to believe it."

"What?"

"Maggots dipped in blackstrap molasses and then coated with brewer's yeast, kelp powder and oat bran."

She backed up a few steps, looking at me as if I were a crackpot.

"Honest." I told her what had happened with the Super Nutro Bombs.

After she had finished laughing, she said, "Only you, Star. It could only happen to you."

"It was all my mother's fault!"

Julie shook her head, then bent down to look at Goldy-legs again. "That web is really amazing. Call me when you're going to test it, OK?"

"OK."

"Promise?"

"OK, OK, I'll call you." I smiled. "Hey, are you turning into an spider fan or something?"

"Of course not!" Julie grinned. "Well, maybe just a little."

"Starshine, look at this," my dad called from the living room.

I came in. He was pointing at the TV. YOUNG EINSTEINS blazed across the screen, and then a voice said, "Welcome to *Young Einsteins*, the quiz show that pits the best and brightest young minds against the hardest questions the encyclopedia has to offer. We have all new contestants this week. Introducing, from the left, Miranda Stockton, Dev Chandra, Mitchell Sorotnik and Tabitha Tan. Ladies and gentlemen, the new Young Einsteins!"

The studio audience clapped. Miranda looked bright and nervous, with a fake smile pasted on her face. Dev looked serious and scared, as though he'd much rather be building solar system models than appearing on TV. Mitchell looked relaxed, a lock of hair falling over one eye. Tabitha — this was the first time I'd seen her — was small for her age. She looked more like seven instead of nine. But she looked tough. She stared defiantly through her glasses as if daring them to give her a question she couldn't answer.

Jack and June started asking questions and the buzzers went off like firecrackers. The square root of 2116 ... the capital of Ghana ... the atomic number of magnesium ... the key products of Greenland. Most times they got the answers right. They just *knew* this stuff. Once Mitchell missed a question — he said there were thirty-six quarts in a bushel instead of thirty-two — and he gave a look as if to say, Darn, I should have known that. But the most amazing one was Tabitha. What a brain! She knew everything. She hit her buzzer like a pistol. Every time she got one right she grinned. It looked as though she was really enjoying herself.

The scores climbed higher and higher. June flipped up a card. "How many teeth does a full-grown bear have?"

"Forty-eight," my dad guessed.

"Fifty-two," I guessed.

BUZZ! Tabitha hit her button. "Twenty-four."

"Correct."

"Holy cow!" my dad said and we laughed.

"You know, I'm glad I didn't make it," I said.

He looked at me. "Really?"

I nodded. "I'm smart, but not like that. I couldn't answer

those questions, especially so fast. I'd be so nervous, I'd probably say all kinds of stupid things."

"Like grizzle?"

I laughed. "Yeah, like grizzle. And blooper." I watched Tabitha answer another one. "She's really having fun. It wouldn't be fun for me."

My dad patted me on the leg. "That's a good thing to know about yourself."

I nodded. There still was an ache inside. It would have been neat to have been on TV, to have felt the cameras pointing at me, to have known that, just for this moment, thousands of people were seeing me. But it was just a little ache. My dad was right. It was good to know that it wouldn't have been worth it if I'd had to do it by pretending to be something I wasn't.

Chapter Twelve

I fed Goldy-legs the last bomb-encrusted maggot. Now the big moment had come.

I called Julie to tell her to come over, but her mom answered and said she wasn't feeling well.

"Would you tell her it's the weigh-in, Mrs. Wong?" I said. "She really wanted to see it."

"OK, Starshine, hold on a minute."

I waited. Mrs. Wong came back. "You'd better go ahead without her, Starshine. She said she'd probably throw up on Goldy-legs."

"Then keep her away!" I said, and her mom laughed. I promised I'd call Julie later and tell her how it went.

I got the weighing posts and the RECORD OF WEB STRENGTH ready — I had to write quite small in the space for "INSECT" to fit in all the ingredients.

The web looked strong and golden yellow. When I came over, Goldy-legs actually moved aside — she was used to the routine by now.

One golf ball ... two golf balls ... three golf balls ... The web didn't even sag.

"Goldy-legs, are you watching this?" I said excitedly.

Seven golf balls ...

Eight ... "I can't look! I can't look!"

One after the other, the balls nestled in. The web stretched but bounced up again.

Eleven ... Same as the moths.

Twelve golf balls. "We broke our record, Goldy-legs!"

Thirteen ...

"Goldy-legs, can you believe this?" I said as I added another.

Fifteen ...

I could hardly bear to look. I could hardly breathe. Carefully, gently, I laid the sixteenth golf ball in the web. That was all the golf balls we had in the house. It held! The web hardly even sagged, it was so strong. The sixteen golf balls sat in there like — like — eggs ... like potatoes ... like groceries!

"Goldy-legs, we did it! We did it!"

I removed the web from the posts and gathered up the corners. It held. It bounced and stretched like elastic, but it held.

I ran inside. "Mom, look! It's the maggots! It's the bombs. Look!"

I bounced the web in front of my mom's face. She grinned. "Well, I'll be! I told you those Super Nutro Bombs delivered a megaton of nutrition, didn't I?"

"You did, you did! Oh, beautiful bombs! Oh, marvelous maggots!"

My mom laughed as I spun her around. "Careful! You don't want the web to rip."

"It won't rip. Look how strong it is. Oh, I bet I'll win the contest, don't you think, Mom?"

"Yes, I'm sure you will," my mom said. "Maggots and bombs — who would have thought?"

I danced around the kitchen. "Oh, I'm so happy you jiggled my arm."

"*I* jiggled *your* arm?" my mom said, coming after me.

I giggled and scooted out of the way.

"By the way, Starshine, have you fed Hughie today?"

"Oops." I'd been so excited about the web, I'd forgotten all about him. "I'll go over right now."

Clutching the precious web in my hand, I skipped down our back steps, through the gap in the hedge that separated our yard from Mrs. Wentworth's, and started up her back steps. After going up the first two steps, I realized Hughie hadn't given me his welcoming bark — he recognizes my footsteps and always barks hello. That was strange. I hurried up the rest of the steps. The door was open a crack. That was even stranger. I was sure I'd locked it the last time I was here. I peeked in the kitchen window. Immediately I drew back. There was a man inside Mrs. Wentworth's house!

I had a moment of panic. But then I thought, He's probably from the electric company or something. Yeah, checking the furnace or reading the meter or whatever they do. I breathed a sigh of relief.

But then why hadn't Mrs. Wentworth told me he was

coming? And what was he doing in the living room?

I peeked in again. That's when I saw Hughie. He was in his basket in the kitchen. There was a red handkerchief around his snout, holding his mouth shut, and a rope around him, tying him into his basket. Even with the handkerchief, Hughie was growling low in his throat. I looked past him to the living room. The man had his back to me. He was standing in front of Mrs. Wentworth's glass-doored cabinet — the one where she kept her silver spoons — and he was shoving the spoons into a cloth bag.

It was the burglar! The silver thief!

My heart started pounding so hard I could hear it in my ears. What was I going to do? I couldn't go in there — maybe he had a gun! I figured I'd better run home and call the police. Yes, that was the only sensible thing to do.

But just then he closed the cabinet door and started turning my way. I ducked beneath the kitchen window. It looked like he was ready to leave. If I ran home now, he'd get away. There wasn't time. I had to hide. But I couldn't let him get away. I had to do something to catch him, and right now. But what? What? Think!

I looked down and realized I still had the web in my hand, with the golf balls in it. An idea popped into my head. A crazy idea. Would it work? Maybe. Maybe not. But it was the only thing I could think of. The clink of spoons coming nearer told me I had no time to waste. As quickly as I could, I put all the golf balls on Mrs. Wentworth's back stairs, a few balls on each step. Then I hid under the stairs with the empty web in my hands, and waited.

The kitchen door opened with a slight squeak and the man said in a sneering voice, "Now you just keep quiet like a good doggie, OK, boy?" He laughed. Hughie growled. I could tell he was miserable being so helpless.

The guy closed the door. He stood on the landing and jiggled the bag. Clinkety-clink went the spoons. "A pretty good haul, even if I do say so myself," he gloated.

You rat! I thought. You dog-tying, spoon-stealing, no-good rat.

He stepped onto the top step. I held my breath. There was a scuffling sound, a rolling sound, and then — "Whah! —" His footsteps tumbled over my head. "— Whuh! —" One golf ball after another bounced to the ground. "— Oh — uh — oh — oh —" Smash! Bam! "— Whoooooo-aaaahhh!" Clatter-bang "Unnnhhh." With a moan he fell at the bottom of the stairs. The bag flew from his hand. I peeked out. He was lying still. The last golf ball rolled to a stop in the grass.

I crawled out from under the steps. My heart pounded as I tiptoed towards him. He looked like he was knocked out cold. He didn't budge. I wasn't taking any chances. I threw Goldy-legs's sticky yellow web over his hands where they lay stretched out on the grass over his head. Then I ran inside and dialed 9-1-1.

"Welcome to the Evening News. In our top story, a local girl becomes a crime-fighting hero with the help of spiders and golf ..."

I was sitting in the living room with my family all around me. The TV announcer smiled out at us.

"A Vancouver schoolgirl, Starshine Shapiro, today helped police nab the notorious silver thief who has been burglarizing Vancouver homes for the past two months. The plucky ten-and-three-quarters-year-old surprised the thief at the home of her next-door-neighbour, Mrs. Olive Wentworth, who was in the hospital following an adenoidectomy. Starshine was looking after Mrs. Wentworth's dog, Hughie, when she apprehended the burglar making away with Mrs. Wentworth's collection of silver spoons."

Then, there I was, in Mrs. Wentworth's kitchen. I was sitting on a kitchen chair and Hughie was resting his chin on my leg, slobbering on my jeans, his tail wagging and slapping the legs of Constable Salim, the police officer, who was standing beside me. There was a smudge on my cheek, probably from when I'd been hiding under Mrs. Wentworth's stairs.

I smiled into the camera. "You see, I was taking part in a scientific experiment to try to strengthen the web of the *Nephila* spider," I explained, holding up the now-torn web. "I have a *Nephila* called Goldy-legs on my back porch, over there —" I pointed off camera. "We've been next-door neighbours with Mrs. Wentworth ever since we moved to Vancouver — and Mr. Wentworth, too, only he died — and ... where was I?"

"The scientific experiment," Constable Salim said.

"Oh, yes. Well, I've been feeding my spider maggots with — with a special nutritional supplement."

"Maggots?" He drew back.

"Mmm-hmm," I said, nodding. "Goldy-legs loved 'em!"

He looked puzzled. "And could you explain, Ms. Shapiro, where the golf balls come in?"

"Well, you see, they were part of the experiment," I said, my eyes roving around the find the camera. I smiled at it. "I had these weighing posts made of Tinker Toys and each week I tested the web to see how many golf balls it would hold. Moths were pretty good. Wasps stunk. But maggots were best. You wouldn't expect that, since *Nephilas* usually prefer flying insects, but maggots were tops. Sixteen golf balls. You want me to run home and get the RECORD OF WEB STRENGTH and show you?"

"Uh, no thanks, that won't be necessary," Constable Salim said.

Then the camera switched to the police removing the web from the thief's hands — it stuck to their fingers and they yanked it off disgustedly — and putting handcuffs on him. He scowled at the camera and muttered, "Caught by a kid with golf balls." He smacked himself in the head with the handcuffs. "Ow!" As they led him away, the news announcer said that he had stolen over five thousand dollars worth of silver, including bowling trophies, jewelry, coins and cutlery.

Then there I was again in Mrs. Wentworth's kitchen.

Constable Salim complimented me on my bravery and cleverness. "Well, it was the only thing I could think of," I said.

Then he smiled and patted me on the shoulder. "Well, Ms. Shapiro, all of Vancouver thanks you for your heroism. And I just want you to know that if you ever decide not to be an arachnologist, there's a place for you on the Vancouver Police Force."

Then Hughie jumped up and licked my face, and we faded off the screen.

"Whoopee!" my dad said, hugging me.

"You're a big hero, Star," Peggy said, sounding awestruck.

"My brave daughter," my mom said in a trembling voice. "I'm so proud. But I swear, Starshine, if you ever do something like that again, I'll —"

"Now, Joanie, let her have her moment of glory."

I just sat there and grinned.

"So, you finally made it onto television," my dad said, ruffling my hair. "How does it feel?"

"Great!" I said.

But as soon as I said it, I knew that wasn't the whole truth. Sure, it was a thrill to be interviewed, to feel the camera focusing on me, to see myself on the screen. But it had also been hot under the lights, and they fussed around so with the clip-on microphones and the camera angles and the powder on my nose. It was such a production. It took forever. I'd just wanted to get home and write up my results and send them in to the American Association of Arachnology. And whip up another batch of Super Nutro Bombs ...

All of a sudden I had an idea. I jumped up from the couch. "Mom, where's that cookbook? With the bomb recipe?"

"In the kitchen. Why?"

"Well, I was thinking. Maybe I could figure out a way to make the bombs even more nutritious. So the web'll be even stronger. I could make *Nephila* basketball nets. Hockey nets. Wouldn't yellow nets look cool on the ice?"

My mom and dad exchanged a look. "Starshine —" my mom began.

"I'll get Fred to breed me a huge colony of maggots," I went on, pacing excitedly back and forth. "Then I'll try changing the recipe. Double the amount of kelp powder. Maybe add tofu. Wow, I can see it now. Volleyball nets. Soccer goal nets. Hammocks! Golden yellow hammocks ..."

If you enjoyed this **Starshine** book, you'll want to read the first two books in the series. Ask your bookseller or librarian for **Starshine!** and **Starshine at Camp Crescent Moon**. Fun-loving Starshine turns everything into an adventure.

Starshine Bliss Shapiro has a problem: her name. What's worse is that she might not go on the grade four camping trip because of a squabble with her parents. But Starshine has a plan involving her hobby — spiders — and the help of her best friend Julie Wong. Now, if only her pesky little sister doesn't foul things up…

Starshine!
0-919591-24-8 • $8.95 Can / $5.95 USA

Starshine is on her way to summer camp, and she's excited — eager for adventure and hopeful about finding a rare spider believed to be extinct. But she's anxious about being homesick, and worried that no one will like her if they find out she has a soft spot for spiders. Adventure and mischief abound!

Starshine at Camp Crescent Moon
0-919591-02-7 • $8.95 Can / $5.95 USA

CEDARLAND SCHOOL
LIBRARY